a simple distance

a novel by

k.e. silva

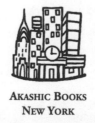

AKASHIC BOOKS
NEW YORK

Published by Akashic Books
©2006 K.E. Silva

ISBN-13: 978-1-933354-11-8
ISBN-10: 1-933354-11-9
Library of Congress Control Number: 2006923121
All rights reserved

First printing

Akashic Books
PO Box 1456
New York, NY 10009
Akashic7@aol.com
www.akashicbooks.com

There's something about an island . . . It gets in your blood.
—George Pascal

Chapter 1

I WAS BORN WITH QUICK-GROWING ROOTS that snuck between my parents and split my family into pieces. As a child I often crept to the top of the staircase that ended just outside my mother's bedroom. I would curl up against its stained picket railing on the last step before our second-floor landing with a blanket and my copy of *The Little Prince*, so I could both read and watch her door.

Whenever I got to the scary part—the chapter on the baobabs—I'd tell myself *it's just a story, the words aren't real*. I'd bend the pages, tear off a small triangle from the corner to assure myself I was in control.

But by then I knew well I'd been born a bad seed, and I'd get stuck, like a scratched record, on particular pages that, no matter what I said, snuck inside and haunted:

> *Now there were some terrible seeds on the planet that was the home of the little prince; and these were the seeds of the baobab.*

The year I started law school, my mom moved back to Baobique. After thirty years in North America, she never stopped calling Baobique home. She'd say it with an air of pride, even superiority, when I was growing up, like having it in her back pocket made her present circumstances bearable. Somewhere else, she was important, had a place more in line with her own image of herself.

It made me feel like she was better than me because she had that other place I barely knew about, when all I ever had was right where I was.

When I was little and she didn't have enough money for groceries, my mom would send me to the market with a list of things to buy and a five-dollar bill. She'd tell me if it wasn't enough money to let the cashier know she'd pay him next time. Then I'd get to the checkout counter and wouldn't have enough money. Everyone in line would stare at me and the cashier would stare at me and none of us knew what to do. Sometimes he'd say it was okay and sometimes he'd make me put things back, but it always felt exactly the same no matter what he did.

Then once I went to the store and only bought the things on the list I knew I could pay for right then. And when I got back to the house and walked up the front steps, the wood exposed under big flakes of paint, white and red; the steps I packed with snow in the winter and made a hill to slide down on my friends' sleds or on those thick "lawn and garden" brown plastic garbage bags; when I got back, I put the groceries on the table and my mom asked where were the rest, and I just looked right back at her. From then on, she only ever sent me with the five-dollar bill. Told me to just get what we needed.

She collects $300 every month from Social Security for working three decades in the States, mostly selling men's clothes at the local department store to our upper-middle-class neighbors, the ones with the sleds and houses whose paint never seemed to flake off like ours, the ones whose parents laid down rules like no building snow ramps on the front steps.

I tried to cover her once through my medical insurance at

work, but my firm said she'd have to be a full dependent. So I only got her supplemental.

Mostly, I live here detached from my mom and my relatives in Baobique. To this day, I keep them curtained off behind a distance as personal as it is geographical. It was Uncle George who first reached through, grabbed me by the ear, and tugged me back; reminded me I could run but never completely hide from who I really was. A Pascal.

My Uncle George was sick an entire year before he died. He was only given a few weeks, but he ended up living with his illness much longer than expected. Leave it to him to break one last bell curve on his way out. The extra time took its toll on the people around him—the ones caring for him up at Granny's those long months. But it gave me a chance to visit him in Baobique—to confront the ghost the island had become to me those years *not visiting* since college, keeping Baobique tucked away at the back of my closet, not admitting how scared I was to reopen its door.

When Uncle George got sick, I had to go. And then Baobique just kept happening.

Nearly a year after my visit to see my sick uncle, I got the call from my mom telling me he'd passed. She'd been with George when he died.

All she spoke of were plums and coconuts. Six a.m. She shouted into the receiver just days after the death of her younger brother: *My plums ripen so slowly. Then, bam! Just like that, they're ready. Have to be picked quick, quick. Otherwise, they'll fall and go to waste. Only good for compost.*

I held the phone a safe few inches from my ear. Or so I'd thought.

She worried, I suppose, that like my late uncle, her voice could no longer be heard by the people around her, and she asked me if, after his funeral, I would fly her to Oakland to recuperate from the loss.

George is dead! George is dead! That's how people told it to each other on Baobique. There, news travels fast. Here, I found out days later when my mom remembered. A forgotten extension of the family tree.

I'd tried to call my grandmother the morning I found out. But she was at the Bato courthouse, freshly whitewashed, just across the narrow street from the sea—a wall of gray brick, built when Britain ran regular ships in and out of the deep-water port, the only thing standing between man and nature. The Chief Justice of the Caribbean held a special session to offer her his condolences about Uncle George. I got through to her that evening as she was watching it on television.

It's a pity you can't be here to see how important your uncle was to this island. Every one else is flying in. They're giving him a state funeral. Just as big as the Prime Minister's last year. Her tone, more formal than ever; she could have been the Chief Justice himself.

My uncle, a conservative who had served as the island's Chief Minister, was buried by the state that week next to his father in our family's plot behind my mother's house.

My mom had hoped the government would offer portable toilets and keep the cars away from her crotons. You never knew where people would walk, or stand, to see such an important man lowered into the earth. She wanted to buy torches, lace them between the small palms lining her drive for my Uncle George, who'd died in her arms. But—what with the plums ripening and everything—it'd slipped her mind.

Just after the funeral, I bought my mom her ticket, free on American Airlines for using my credit card so much. Eating out.

I told her point blank when I gave it to her: *Now that you've got this ticket, you can't change it. You'll have to stick to the plan.* I was stern because I knew being nice would come back to me down the road in the form of a problem, a tightly jumbled knot of changed dates and destinations that only I would be able to unravel.

I cannot think of a single thing I hate more in this world than unraveling my mother's knots. She's never been very gentle with mine. When I was little and we lived outside Chicago, in our run-down Victorian, the one the town kept telling us to paint because my mom and I were bringing down the property values in the neighborhood, she would take the comb to my hair in her unyielding hands as if it wasn't like hers at all, all kinky and twisted and riddled with tangles that yanked at my scalp if not treated with just the tiniest bit of care. So I learned how to braid on my own.

I was supposed to call her the day before she left. Instead I slept, read a book, rifled through a stack of old letters marked with a stamp by the post office: *CHANGE OF ADDRESS REQUESTED*. It was overcast in Oakland; a good day to rest.

The ring from her call burst in my apartment.

Jean! I'm so glad I caught you. I've been trying to reach you since yesterday.

I lied. *Sorry, Mom. I had to buy an air mattress. It took me awhile to find the right type.*

That's what I want to talk to you about. I need you to change my tickets. I've got to visit Aunt Lillian in England.

Mom, I can't do that. Your flight leaves tomorrow. It's too late. I told you when I booked the tickets, they're non-refundable.

Well, that's ridiculous. I've got to see Lil. She has a heart condition. Just tell them. I'm sure they'll make an exception.

Fine, I lied again, *I'll call the airline.*

Chapter 2

CRISIS IS NEVER CONVENIENT. My mom's need to leave Baobique after Uncle George's funeral, to rest from all the care he'd needed—the special food, the midnight cleanings, the patience—coincided almost to the day with what was to be the biggest hearing of my yet undistinguished legal career.

I think my boss felt he owed me when he assigned me Cynthia's case. The last case we had worked on together had a number of plaintiffs out of state, entailed a lot of traveling in the rural South, a place with which neither of us had much experience. He was a sort of rising star at our firm: sandy-blond hair, Yale law. Just a few years my senior.

The only advice we got was to make sure, *make damn sure,* everyone knew we were *not* a couple. He should expose his wedding band, talk about his wife back home often enough to alleviate any threat of our possible union.

We played along, let people assume I was his secretary, his helper, not co-counsel; didn't correct their natural assumptions of what a brown-skinned woman and a white-skinned man should, rightly, have been doing together. It put them at ease, got us the information we wanted, when I pretended to be something I wasn't.

Sometimes he'd slip: refer to me as co-counsel. Sometimes I'd slip: stand erect, head high, shoulders relaxed, and walk next to him, instead of the choreographed few steps behind. In the car, rented in his name, he behind the wheel driving to the next destination on our list, I'd take my frustration out on him, snap at him for a wrong turn, a disagreement in strategy, a smoke break; tell him he was slowing us down, imply he was pampered, lazy.

For stretches of time we'd say nothing, apologizing to each other for things we couldn't help with small silences. Back at the hotel, I'd slam my feet into my sneakers, yank on my shorts, grab my room key, and run on the treadmill until my legs felt like rubber, until my gasps for breath disrupted the boy at the counter watching MTV.

It's fitting, really, when you think about it—me, so grudgingly coming to the aid of my own mother, flying her in after the death of her younger brother—being assigned to represent Cynthia in her child custody case. Cynthia's ex-lover, Linda, was suing her for joint custody of their daughter. Sadie was four and Linda, her other mother.

The first time we met, Cynthia, still physically shaken, hands trembling from the recency of the shock, let go our formal roles and told me things more fit for friend than lawyer. She told me how messy things had gotten.

Linda had moved from their flat but left her things behind: her bed, her couch, the kitchen table. Only took underwear, bras, and extra shoes. She had a thing for shoes. They had to match her socks and belt and the trim of her gay-boy shirts.

Cynthia'd told her to leave and to take the dog. She'd developed asthma from the dander of an animal in the house.

At first, I'd tried to refocus the discussion. I told her, *Cynthia, I need for you to clarify what you want to achieve from this process.*

But Cynthia wasn't easily led. *I need her to answer for this thing I'm left with. This thing of everything to nothing in a single day,* she'd said. That wasn't what I meant and she knew it but continued any-way. *Linda said it had been building for months, her feelings for Cara, but she'd only just realized it now.*

Resigned to Cynthia's insistence on things emotional, I ceased interrupting. Just listened.

She told me she loved me a lot. And then she took it back. Said it wasn't true, ever, and that now she had it with someone else.

Cynthia had gone through Linda's photographs from before they met. The ones Linda'd never let her see, in the red box on the highest shelf so only Linda—six feet tall and go-go-gadget arms—could reach. She was a compulsive photographer of social events. Everything to look like a party. Cynthia hated that, so Linda only ever took pictures of Sadie and the dog.

Cynthia had pulled up a chair—Linda's, red vinyl from the kitchen table—and brought it down. Dividers the size of index cards, pink and blue, separated the stages of Linda's life. Three or four past girlfriends. The one that wouldn't talk to her anymore, who frothed lattes into pictures across the street from their flat, naked from the waist up, at some lake. Linda behind her in the next one, bare as well. Nipples a dull gray from the low contrast of the black-and-white film, and protruding toward each other—almost touching. Lots of kissing with her different girls. Cynthia made me look. She was scared she would vanish altogether because she was nowhere in that box.

She's turned off her cell phone to avoid my ring, but I leave messages. I've told her she needs to get her things out. I can't sleep in our bed.

Linda's things were to go from the house, leaving it empty.

The air in my lungs, Jean . . . Now that the dog's gone, there's nothing else inside.

I had to cut in. *What about Sadie?* A reminder, not a correction.

She sighed. *And Sadie.* Back. *Of course, Sadie. Always.*

That was all she needed. Ready, then, to move forward with the real purpose of our discussion.

At the time, the law on the issue was in a state of flux.

Later, the day before my mom arrived, I asked Cynthia to stop by my office. A new appellate decision had strengthened her claim considerably. *This decision*, I told her, *will likely mean the difference of sole, instead of joint, custody of your daughter.*

We had been discussing the upcoming hearing. Until this new decision, we'd prepared for a fight, tough but fair. I'd prepared Cynthia for the likelihood of joint custody; the rule that would guide the judge's decision being the *best interests* of Sadie.

But the California Court of Appeal, the court that says what goes until the State Supreme Court says otherwise, had up and changed the game. Second-parent adoption, they said, was no longer valid. Not being the birth mother, Linda suddenly had no rights.

The court had just handed my client a royal flush. It was as if I'd been given all the answers to the questions on my final exam a week early.

But that wasn't what I'd wanted to do with my life. Harm. To me, it seemed we should still be guided by Sadie's *best interests*, set adult feelings aside. I asked just to check, *How's Sadie?*

Cynthia's long stare out the window was a pretty good indication. That morning she'd pushed Sadie on her bicycle, new with training wheels; feet up, on the handlebars, away from the pedals so they wouldn't get caught in the revolutions. Sadie'd said to her, *Push me so fast I can't even stand it!* Cynthia's hand on Sadie's back, she'd pushed the girl faster than was safe because too much had already been denied her child. She couldn't add to the list.

Sadie had started to get sick all on her own: ran fevers and took to bed, sweat through the night and soaked her sheets.

Cynthia learned her patterns, left fresh night shirts by her pillow in case Sadie wanted to start over in the middle of the night.

She's fine until she sees Linda, Cynthia told me. *But when they're together, and then Linda leaves . . . It's like reopening a wound. Different every time.*

Days prior, Sadie had sat silently in the front window, curled up into a ball, rocking herself back and forth. Cynthia had pulled the girl to her lap on the couch, and they rocked together, watching the ocean, its disappearing white lines, until sunset. The waves grown taller with winter. Other times, Sadie just screamed and screamed. Screeching at the top of her lungs as Linda drove away. Threw herself against the window, slapping palm to pane.

What could I say? I said nothing.

Jean?

Yes, Cynthia?

What are we doing to my daughter?

Chapter 3

MY MOTHER CALLED ME again the morning she was supposed to leave Baobique, but I didn't pick up. I cursed the three-hour time difference—her ring waking me before my coffeemaker could ease me into morning the way I preferred. Just before the opening, closing, slamming doors of my next-door neighbor readying and leaving, Procter & Gamble usually anticipated my most basic of needs, had something ready for me like a silent, supportive partner. Programmable, twenty-five dollars secondhand off the Internet: unconditional love. The touch of the spoon against the inside of my mug, the reassuring clink as I stirred in too much sugar, too much cream.

I ignored her ring, lay in bed on the verge of getting up, pulling on shorts, starting the day with a jog and some music on my Walkman, but her second call caught me off guard—changed my plans.

I picked up to her raspy *Hello.*

She spoke in that low voice of hers, the one that says, *I'm weak, take care of me,* the one that makes me want to scream, the one she used all those years she lay in bed without actually being sick, with her *Reader's Digest* condensed classics and jug, always a jug, of cheap white wine, stretching the telephone cord long beyond its intended curl. I know because all those years I sat at the top of the front stairs just outside her door, and watched.

She whispered, *I've packed my bags and had Fatima put them in the Jeep. I was waiting for your call about England. Were you able to change the tickets?*

I hated her for needing me; hated her double for choosing me second, over Auntie Lil in London; hated myself most for feeling this way.

Never having called the airline, I continued to lie. *No, Mom. The airline wouldn't let me change them. You can't visit Aunt Lillian. I'm sorry. She'll have to fend for herself this time.*

Hollow, like a ghost giving in, she agreed. *Okay, Jean. I'll see you tomorrow. I'll call Lillian when I reach you.*

My mom told me once how kids used to tease her, call her wide hips the spreading baobab tree, pretend to take their shelter there. Yet those hips never sheltered me, and when it came my turn to do the blocking, to break the wind, call the airline, to soften the violence of its impact before it reached her small body; when it came my turn, I stood as thin as possible beside her, closed my eyes, held my breath, hoped it would just blow through.

That morning I lay in bed longer than planned, remembered a time when I was five and sick to my stomach. I had called for my mom to come help, not even help really, but just to come and maybe hold my hand. I remembered she called back from her bedroom and she said: *Oh, just do it yourself, child.*

That morning I did not rise. Stared across the room at unanswered letters.

I picked her up at the gate. American Airlines, flight 2330. Baobique to Puerto Rico; Puerto Rico to Houston; Houston to San Francisco. Three legs to my mother's journey away from her home, to mine, to rest after a year of caring for her dying brother.

As always, she had too many bags: an overnight case; two large paper shopping bags, handles tied together with twine; her purse, overstuffed. The steward helped her off the plane only to hurry her along.

Her eyes were red like the blood in those oranges whose name she used to write on the grocery lists I could never completely purchase. She was shorter, her neck more rounded, than the last time I'd seen her. It took me aback.

Oh my God! What's the matter with your eyes?

Here, take my bags from that man and give him a dollar.

We hugged, leaned in with just our shoulders, embraced with just our forearms; pressed our cheeks together, left as much space as possible in between.

I took her luggage from the steward. Tipped him. Moved on to baggage claim.

On the drive home, her bags in both the backseat and the trunk of my Mazda, as if each day of her scheduled three-week stay would require a distinct new outfit, she told me about her eyes. *It's the stress that's making me sick. Ever since George's funeral. All those people on the porch one on top of the other, touching all my things . . . They tried to let them in the house, you know. My house! As if I had no say in the matter at all. Mama acts as if Godwyn isn't even mine.*

Well, the title's joint, Mom. You both have equal say.

Jean, I've spent the past nine years in that house! The only reason Mama wants it now is because of what I've made of it. She started to cough.

After the funeral she had lain in bed for two days, head throbbing, throat swollen and closing in on itself every time she swallowed, lungs too heavy to push all the air out, but chest too burdened to resist the exhale. Her right eye had turned red, perhaps from the exertion of pushing out the yellow mucus her head and lungs were trying to clear. Then, her left. The nurse, at the hospital named after my grandfather, said the redness was bacterial, gave her antibiotic drops to be used every four hours.

When my mom first returned to Baobique, Godwyn was practically abandoned. My grandfather, buried out back, who walked its rooms at night, was the favorite story of my cousins. To her nieces and nephews, my mom would say the ghost of her father only protected her. To her brothers, she admitted being frightened by the isolation of the house, just up the hill from Sommerset, its rough characters and drug smuggling, and not within sight, or earshot, of even a single neighbor. So Uncle Martin gave her the best bitch from his second litter. And Uncle George bought her a little handgun, like the kind my aunt shot her son-in-law with when he was beating my cousin. My mom kept it underneath her pillow when she slept, even though she never learned to use it.

Everyone thought she was crazy to move in. But later my cousins would come 'round asking about her health, hoping she'd pass before Granny, lose her hold on land they wanted to claim as their own inheritance, not hers.

The driveway, closely cut grass, she lined with yellow and green crotons. The approach to the house, small palms, just beginning to demand notice. The backdrop to the west, the Atlantic. And to the east, Morne Volcan, my mother's strength— the mountain she's looked to for anchor since she was a child. Volcan is covered in rainforest, shrouded in mist, bigger and more aware of its position than any other mountain on the small island. Her back porch, off the kitchen, looks at Volcan, as if to keep the mountain secret, while the eyes of visitors look toward the ocean from the public front.

Much of the estate is cliff, but parts are level enough for planting. So while her family, the Pascals, weren't using the land, people from Sommerset, the village down the road, were.

They set up gardens.

Technically, they were supposed to pay rent to Uncle George, but the payments had never been strictly enforced because Sommerset was an important constituency of his. When my mom moved in, she decided the gardeners should start paying. The gardeners, however, thought otherwise.

Back then, my mom had a woman from Sommerset, Mrs. H, come up to help every day with the washing and cooking. Mrs. H's husband sometimes came around to spray the fruit trees with pesticides banned in North America and to clear away underbrush. The first report of how the gardeners felt about paying rent came from Mrs. H, who'd heard it from her husband. Rumor had it that some of the men in Sommerset thought my mom was being quite presumptuous to come back to Baobique after thirty years, stay all alone at Godwyn, and tell them to pay rent for land they had been using for long before her return. Some of those men thought they should go up there late one night and *teach dat 'oman a lesson, na*, rough her up like only a man could. The rumor was repeated to my mom by the old man with the apple-core head who used to sleep in her shed at night in exchange for dinner; an arrangement which gave him food and shelter and gave my mom a second presence on the estate when she was asleep and most vulnerable.

Turned out to just be a rumor though. Unsettling only because it came from Sommerset.

My studio sat half a block from one of those trendy Bay Area streets, like 24th Street or Castro in San Francisco; 4th Street in Berkeley; mine being Piedmont in Oakland, and the whiteness of the walls offered me a blank slate of which I appeared to be in particular need.

It occurred to me, as I drove my mother home, that I had yet to place anything on those walls, and while for so long their lack of clutter had perhaps provided me with a certain solace, they had now turned into something of a little pebble fallen in my shoe that rubbed and rubbed and rubbed against my skin. I knew the walls would strike her as freakish. Again I'd be the odd duck, a failure at all things feminine, like simple decoration and sleeping with men.

I turned into the tight driveway that separated my building from the next, parked in the dirt under the lemon tree in back, not really a spot but big enough for my practical hatchback.

Jean, you'll have to back up for me to get out. I'm right in the dirt here.

I backed up, let her out on the cement, re-parked, and began unloading her bags as she walked up to the back door; the curve of her neck, more pronounced than ever before, made her look older than merely middle-aged.

Here, Mom, I'll let you in. You must be tired.

I unlocked the door for her, returned to the luggage as she disappeared inside.

By the time I'd carried in the last of her belongings, she was asleep on my futon, still folded into a couch. That night, I slept on the air mattress.

Chapter 4

S HE WOKE ME PLACING HER BAGS one by one by one on my creaky futon, though I lay still a minute before I mumbled, *Morning*, wiped the sleep from my eyes, and rose from the air mattress.

She'd done that to me all my life. When I was a teenager, she'd vacuum right outside my bedroom door weekend mornings when she thought it was time for me to get up and get to work on something or another.

I mustered up maturity.

Jean, she said, *why haven't you done anything with these walls? I feel I'm in an insane asylum.*

Irritated, I ignored her, retreated to the bathroom for an inordinately long time, washing my hair squeaky-clean; wondering if we couldn't, maybe, catch a double-feature that afternoon at the theater down the street; kicking myself for not thinking— scheduling her arrival to fall on a weekend instead of a weekday when I'd have a reason to be at work.

Perhaps I had no excuse to be acting like such a child. But her being in my space, it all came back. Ours was an uneasy reunion.

Everything would be fine if we could just speak to each other as little as possible.

I was thinking about a movie later, Mom. Maybe a double-feature, down the street.

I didn't tell her the only double-feature was back-to-back *Star Wars*: the last one, and then the prequel. She might have balked.

The movie didn't start until 2:00, but it was hard enough spending the entire morning locked in my studio with her, unpacking and unpacking and unpacking for what seemed like forever, her clothes taking up more of my closet than mine. Every five minutes commenting on my absence of décor.

So we bought our tickets right after lunch. I figured we'd wait out the last forty-five minutes standing first in line at the theater.

But I hadn't figured on running into anyone. My heart stopped for just a second when I saw walking toward us on the same side of the street as our nonexistent queue: Linda, my client Cynthia's ex, and their daughter Sadie—the subject of the custody battle. Hand in hand.

Neither of them knew my face. Cynthia kept Sadie far away from our firm, wanting her to be around as little conflict as possible regarding the suit. And there'd been no reason for us to meet with Linda as yet. The hearing was still a week away and any attempts at negotiation would not likely happen until just before. There was nothing for them to recognize in me, although I felt I knew them both intimately from my meetings with Cynthia and the family photos in her file.

My stomach started to tighten. More than I'd realized from Sadie's photos, there in person, by both looks and predicament, she could have been me at her age. They had gotten the sperm from an international bank and didn't know much about Sadie's father, only those things he chose to report—ordinary illnesses, education, race. A Jamaican intellectual with a predisposition toward melancholy.

* * *

The night before my father left, I caught them. I'd pulled off my thin cotton sheet to get out of bed, stepped to the creaky wooden floor, walked only in the places I knew wouldn't give me away—close to the walls—and moved toward their voices. Down the hallway and the dark back stairs. My breathing short. My eyes wide.

The door to the kitchen, at the bottom of the stairs, was ajar. Just enough.

My mom was pressed up against the sink, plates stacked precariously by her side. Earlier that evening she'd made me pull up a chair, like always, so I could reach the faucet and wash the dinner dishes, but I hadn't taken care to place them properly in the rack. She wore a white nightshirt and her skin was glowing through it, dark and red, under the florescent light from the ceiling.

My dad was there too, holding a belt in his right, dominant fist, looped like a teardrop. They were saying things, blurry whispers short and angry, more like spitting than speaking. But their words came to me strange, like the flapping of a flock of autumn birds flying south: starting far away, their wings only loud for the second they passed, and then quiet. So all I really heard, for sure, was the clear, crisp slapping.

There, on the stairs, the consequences of my next step in either direction, backward into the dark or forward into the kitchen, held me still.

Maybe if I'd taken more care to sturdy the dishes as I'd placed them to dry, we all could have pretended it never happened. Maybe it was my dad's fault for pushing her too close to the rack, or hers for letting him. But something happened, some part of them bumped up against it, and all at once, everything came crashing down—all of dinner's dishes, along with my mom, landing hard and broken on the floor in front of the sink. And it was one of those screams that was halfway out before I realized it was me. So I couldn't take it back.

Both of their eyes, my father's and my mother's, caught mine as my dad raised his arm again. And the awareness that his fist was in a place it shouldn't have been obscured its purpose for just a moment. But then it came down—again and again and again; their eyes never leaving mine.

The next day, he left us in his old pea-green Mustang.

I was waiting for my father to pick me up for the weekend the first time I realized I was black. I was standing in the downstairs bathroom, wearing red hand-me-down Garanimals from my sometimes best friend Becky: elastic-waisted pants crawling with fruit trees and monkey faces; plain red shirt, turtlenecked for a cold fall, thin frills at the wrists and just below my chin.

It was never warm enough in our house. My mom would set the thermostat at fifty-five degrees and call it the *comfort zone*. But I knew better. I never felt comfortable in that house. I used to sit, knees to chest, in front of the metal vents when the temperature fell to fifty-four and the forced air clicked itself on.

On really frigid days in winter, I'd fill the sink with water, hot from the tap, keep my sleeves rolled down to my wrists, and soak my hands and forearms until the blood under my puckered skin came closer to the surface. Then I'd sit in front of the vents, because they warmed me even better when my shirt was wet. The water, I learned, had a way of conducting the heat more directly to my body than just plain air.

It was one of those days: bitter cold, made colder by the crack in my father's broken promise to come get me, letting in the outside air sure as any open door. I'd waited for him since after school, had come straight home.

I always waited for my dad about three feet off the ground, on the ledge of our big picture window in the living room that framed my world: the tall oak across the street, whose lower-hanging branches I'd climb and swing on; the wire fence that separated our house from the old peoples' home next door; the mulberry trees on the other side of that fence, in easy reach after scaling the links, their fruit bursting dark, fat, and purple on the branches; the blue jays that flew into the glass when it was too clean and the sun reflected only clouds and sky; the three strips of gray concrete my dad put in as a driveway before the divorce, two for the wheels, one for walking, running parallel to our house, where the green Mustang used to rest before he took it with him and my mom started renting parking space to help with the mortgage. That mortgage with the special rate because our town had been told, just before we got there, to increase its efforts at integration.

But I didn't make it to the heater that day. Or to the ledge. That day, as I turned to open the bathroom door—wet sleeves and wrinkly hands making their way to the white porcelain knob—the mirror, half-broken from one of my parents' fights, left off the top half of my reflection. So it was my hands, belly-high, that stopped me: brown hands against that white knob. It was right there in the mirror. The contrast.

I thought maybe that was why my dad forgot so often to come pick me up when it was his turn. Maybe he was mad at me for coming out like her. And maybe that was why my mom stayed in her room all the time, door closed to my face, reminding her too much of her own. Maybe I'd failed them both, coming out the way I did.

I was in the first grade and just getting accustomed to that idea when I met Mr. Walker, came to find out I wasn't black enough at all. He had some of the big kids drag me, literally, upstairs to the second floor, where he was sitting on his stool in his classroom: a king surrounded by his subjects, waiting for the offering of my small body. Mr. Walker was the only black teacher at Lincoln. Ever. He was a very large man.

After the big kids pried off my banana hat, long and yellow with a green loop on top for hanging, Mr. Walker took one look at me and smiled a great, big Cheshire cat smile, the one he'd wear for years to come, every time he saw me, all the way up from the first grade to the sixth, when he recruited me into his class. If nothing else, he was a patient man.

Even when I was in his class, every day looking at his face, nothing about Mr. Walker felt familiar to me like he thought it was supposed to. He would have our class read books out loud about African-Americans and slavery in the South, and I learned it right along with all the little white suburban kids in my class, but it never hit home. Not really. We learned *cotton* and *Confederates,* ignored *cane* and *Caribbean* and other such things that would have helped me make sense of my hands and their history when I looked in our half-broken mirror.

One day, Mr. Walker kept me back from music class—where Ms. Costa, the music teacher, would sit us in a circle, play "Kumbaya," "Michael Row Your Boat Ashore," on her acoustic guitar, and we'd sing along to mimeographed lyrics—to tell me about the way the world was. He sat me down in someone else's desk, pulled his stool up close. He told me junior high was going to be different; there'd be black kids there and I'd have a very hard time if I didn't start hanging out with them. Told me I'd need to switch sides.

There'd never been any other side at Lincoln. And all those books we'd read out loud doing nothing but making me feel like I really belonged somewhere else—I wasn't so sure the black kids would want me on their side in junior high.

My eyes were still red from crying when everyone else came back from music. So they all knew something big had happened. When they asked me what it was, I just sat there speechless, in whoever's desk.

Sometimes I dreaded the color of my skin because it made Mr. Walker single me out, fixate on me and the salvation of my sixth-grade soul, when all I ever wanted to do was hide. He thought I wasn't being taught at home to be black enough. So after his talk with me, he called in my mom, made her miss an afternoon of work we couldn't afford, and gave her the same talk for which he'd held me back from music. Perhaps he even made her sit in the same desk.

My mom may not have been a book, but I'm pretty sure she read herself out loud to Mr. Walker that day. *Who in God's name* was this crazy, fat man to tell her she'd raised her daughter wrong?

Before that day, Mr. Walker hadn't a clue that beneath the chipped paint of our porch stairs, her department-store job selling clothes we couldn't buy ourselves, and our five-dollar trips to the grocery store, ran the blood of Pascal arrogance that matched his own step for step. She told him point blank: *West Indians are not American.* She's never been a diplomat.

I shut my eyes, held my breath, kept still as possible for the rest of the year. And he never held me back from music class again.

Pity, my mom said to me once, *pity you didn't get your father's coloring. It's a dark child sees dark days.*

Cynthia and Linda never registered as domestic partners. So when Cynthia gave birth to Sadie, there was never any way to bind them all, by statute, as family. Only by contract was it possible to make Linda Sadie's mother, through a second-parent adoption agreement.

Improvisation. Doing, simply, the best they could, second-parent adoption afforded them a chance to assert what the law would have liked to forget: that each family was different. For fifteen years, in California, second-parent adoptions had been the only choice for gay and lesbian couples. Our contracts carried our intent because no other rule would.

I let Linda and Sadie pass, averted my eyes. Yet they were all I saw, my mother's voice yammering on and on about something I'd stopped listening to minutes ago.

Sometimes my ethics as a lawyer ran counter to my ethics as a human being. And the thing I hated most was my first thought—that I should speak with Cynthia about limiting Linda's time with Sadie until custody and visitation were settled.

Precedent changing so fast back then, who knew? Holding yourself out to be a child's parent in line for *Star Wars* might have been good enough for a court to agree. Linda acting like Sadie's mother might have convinced a judge she still was.

They bought their tickets and stood in line right behind us. I could barely breathe.

Chapter 5

MONDAY WAS A NEW DAY. I bussed into work, told my mom I'd come home early so we could walk around the lake and catch an early dinner.

My bus began its route across the bay and into the city. A passenger, I looked to the hills, slouched low in my seat as we approached the bridge; took refuge in temporary suspension between where I'd been and where I needed to go.

In Baobique, when you look to the mountains, all you see are trees, tall and arching in the wind, their uppermost fronds green and, perhaps, slick with rain; at night, maybe two or three houses with electric lights, unless you are down south in the capital, Bato, where they have known for quite some time how to work the politics, get themselves things like running water and electricity.

In Bato, at night, looking up at its hills is like what it must have been to look up at Oakland long ago, barely dotted with lights. But during the day I saw no such similarity.

As the bus climbed the bridge, I could see the Golden Gate, the Pacific just beyond, and my mind left my mother's ocean for mine.

Just beyond the cliffs at Fort Point was where Cynthia and Linda bought their house, when Sadie was due. Three pieces of a once solid whole.

As the bus descended the downward slope of the bridge and we reached San Francisco, I wondered what was so wrong with the concept of sharing; why the law so loved the mutually exclusive. I deboarded heavy of foot, crossed the street, and made my way inside.

I remembered a recent telephone conversation with Cynthia, her anger still palpable as she told me, *I saw it coming, you know, Linda and Cara. But I shut my eyes.* She'd hoped it would pass on its own. Linda and Cara were coworkers, saw each other every day in the halls, at meetings. Things like that. Then it'd become social: pot luck dinners, office lunches. Linda would put it on Sadie. She'd say, *Kids aren't really going to be there.* So it was better if Sadie and Cynthia stayed at home.

Cara'd grown bold. Calling Linda's cell phone at home to invite her out on the weekend, putting Linda on the spot. *How can kids not be allowed to go swimming on a Saturday afternoon at Lake Chabot?* Cynthia would ask.

Of course I knew. I knew before Linda, she said. Continued, *Weeks after she left, I thought I'd lose my mind with anger. My neck, my arms, my hands—I burned rage. I called their office, but I didn't know Cara's last name, so I couldn't get past the damn voicemail. I wrote her letters, but again, no last name—so I couldn't send them. I steamed.* Stuck, alone with her righteousness. *I wanted Cara to know that Sadie and I were real and their actions had consequences outside themselves.*

But Linda'd checked out.

Linda wants what she wants. There's nothing I can do about that. But I want what I want, too. And I want her to regret her choice.

I'm sorry, Cynthia, I'd said, trying to offer comfort, but not too much. It was selfish of Linda and Cara, it was. It sounded hard, but look at Cynthia, at what she was doing—using Sadie to see Linda hurt—who was she to talk?

You don't need to take a right from one person to grant it to another. I wished Cynthia could see that. But that week, she had the law on her side and could have taken us back over a decade if she chose.

I grabbed a quick cup of coffee, lots of cream, lots of sugar, passed the receptionist's desk in the kitchenette down the hall from my office, logged on to my computer, pulled up the decision: *Sharon S.*:

> *Annette F. petitioned under the independent adoption statutes to adopt Joshua, the biological son of her relationship partner, Sharon S. (the petitioner here). After the women severed their relationship, Sharon sought to terminate the adoption proceedings, arguing in part that the adoption statutes do not permit a second-parent, or co-parent, adoption (one in which the unmarried relationship partner of the parent adopts that child and the parent retains parental rights). We agree . . .*

The rules that govern our actions derive from conflict. What *Sharon S.* meant was, if you were gay, and you and your partner wanted to parent a child in California, you did so at your own risk. A single paragraph withheld from unmarried couples and their children that which married couples took for granted: family, legally recognized.

And at the end of that week, mine was to be the mouth that made this happen. I cleared my throat, thought about grade school and autumn, when the leaves on the gingko tree in the courtyard of Frank Lloyd Wright's home and studio, kitty corner across Chicago Avenue from the playground, would be yellow and falling to the ground. Thirty-two years old and I was in the fourth grade all over again.

It was at the side of the long, low brick wall protecting the yard from the likes of us, that Sally Johnson first called me a *jungle-bunny*.

Then there was the time in first grade, early spring because my birthday is in May—May 18, Peace Day on the calendar, and also the day Mount St. Helens erupted and we learned for the first time that there were volcanoes in America—that Meghan Callahan, for a joke, sang "Happy Birthday" to me at recess, back behind the dodge ball circle, and when it got time to sing my name, instead of singing, *Happy Birthday to Jean,* she sang, *Happy Birthday to the black girl, Happy Birthday to you*. As if I didn't even have a name.

Until Margaret in the fourth grade, I was the only black student at Lincoln School. Abraham Lincoln Elementary School.

Margaret was in my class. She was tall and thin and almost ran faster than me, even though everyone knew I was the fastest kid at Lincoln, period. Faster, even, than any of the boys in both the fifty-yard dash and all the way around the block. But Margaret didn't know that. She was new. So she kept trying to beat me in the fifty-yard dash, and it got me angry because sometimes she almost did, and she didn't seem to know when to quit. Margaret moved into the duplex next to Sally Johnson's, on Forest, just off Chicago Avenue, right across the street from Wright's home and studio.

When the tourists walked the area with their portable tape players and headsets, they'd go past the other Wright houses, but they'd stop inside his studio. We'd sell them lemonade on the corner in the summer.

Then one day Margaret wasn't at school. She just stopped showing up. Sally said Margaret's front lawn had a cross burned on it with fire, and that Margaret's family had moved away immediately. Right when Sally said it, I knew it was her brothers who'd burned that cross.

I just couldn't figure out why. Why they'd never done that to us; why Sally and I were friends, her parents feeding me lunch sometimes, once even inviting me up to their cabin, the one they built themselves by hand, all the way up in Northern Wisconsin, even though Sally didn't tell me where they all took poops at night and when I stepped right in the middle of some, Sally and her brothers and her dad all just laughed. I thought maybe they hadn't burned a cross on our lawn because we didn't move in right next door to them. We were all the way on the other side of the block. Or maybe they hadn't burned a cross on our lawn because my dad looked white, or because I was friends with Sally, or because our moms were friends.

But I never could figure it out. And I sort of felt like I had something to do with Margaret leaving, like I should have pro-tected her or something because her skin was just like mine. And even though I'd never really liked her, wished she'd given up on the fifty-yard dash business like everyone else, when she left it felt scary, like I was all alone.

I printed out the *Sharon S.* case, tossed it on the top of Cynthia's file, and left for the day, catching the bus back to Oakland stuck somewhere between disgust and despair. Because when one of us gets burned, we all scar. And right then, I was the one holding the match.

Chapter 6

PERHAPS MY MOTHER WAS EXPECTING a signal, my small gray hatchback to turn into the drive, because she startled when I unlocked the front door. She was talking on the phone, sitting on the futon and watching the side window, which would have allowed her to see my car pull in, if only I had driven instead of taken the bus.

How can you defend her, Lillian? What she's done to me. It's as if she doesn't care about her own mother! Oh look, she just walked in. I should go . . . All right, I will. You take care too, dear.

Tell Auntie Lillian I say hello, Mom.

Jean says hello . . . All right, I will. Bye, dear.

My mother always calls long distance on other people's phones because she can't afford it herself. I had no idea how long she'd been on, but the fact that she couldn't afford to talk with Aunt Lillian, her godmother in England, for hours on end, I'm sure, would not have prevented her from doing so on my dime.

I'd always thought Aunt Lillian was related to us by blood, but she isn't. Even though she lives in Europe, she's one of those people who's always around. At least in conversation. She trained as a nurse in England during World War II. They say she had a fiancé back then, a Baobiquen pilot in the Royal Air Force. But he didn't survive the war.

Baobique's no place for a young woman disinterested in the rest of its men. I guess she thought she was better off where she was. So she stayed in London, worked in a hospital, bought a flat, earned herself a pension.

Normally, I would have commented on the cost of the call. Normally, that would have been bothering me most.

But I was more upset by the substance of the conversation I walked in on than I was its length.

Were you two talking about me?

Well, of course. You're my daughter.

Something was going on and I wanted, more than anything, not to find out what it was. I did not want to wind up in the middle. But I was angry.

Mom, what were you saying about me? For Christ's sake, I just flew you up here. How can you say I don't care about my own mother? What the hell is going on?

Jean, there's no need to get nasty on top of it all.

Mom, I don't even know what I'm getting nasty about! Tell me, specifically, what is going on.

You know exactly what's going on, Jean. This is all your doing. Mama's telling Lillian it's because of that damn goat. What do they think I am, na, a fool? She pressed her tongue to the back of her front teeth, made that sucking noise she only started doing since she returned to Baobique. A noise well below her family's station on the island, a noise that would have sent my grandmother to an early grave. But right then, that was just what my mother would have liked to do.

When I was in Baobique visiting my sick uncle, about a year before his death and my mother's trip to Oakland to recuperate, her dogs killed the goat of a man named Mr. Williams. He worked for her picking seed nuts from the coconut trees at Godwyn to sell in town for three dollars apiece at Saturday market. But when I was there, it was the plums that needed picking.

Mr. Williams had a bum leg, so he couldn't pick the plums. He'd hurt it the day before on the estate, twisted it tripping over a root from some tree that couldn't keep itself entirely underground. My mom and I had to drive him home in her jeep, down the road to Sommerset, where both the ocean and the people are rough but where we managed to accomplish the following things: bought a flat of eggs for bread pudding; gave condolences to a woman whose father had recently died from drinking a jug of lye; said hello to Mr. Issacs, Uncle George's secretary's father, and to another older, balding man whose connection to my relatives I've forgotten. People gathered in the little intersection as my mom's car blocked the road and we talked.

At one point, four young men walked by eyeing me, as most of the men there do to all women under forty. They looked me up and down, hung out in front of our car until my mom honked them to the side. It was obvious they didn't like us, with our car, our house, our maid, while so many people lived in shacks. There was one man in particular who scared me, his right eyelid sewn shut, who wouldn't look away even as we rolled by.

Next morning, bright and early, Rascal and Lucia started barking. Like mad dogs at the bottom of the plum tree. My mom told me to grab her cutlass from the kitchen wall, so I did. And we went to investigate.

When we got to the dogs, we looked up and saw two sets of brown eyes staring down at us from among the plums. But it wasn't the men from Sommerset, it was Mr. Williams's two sons, come to steal what they could off the tree bursting with fruit.

They told us they were just there to see about their father's goat; that Rascal and Lucia had chased them up the tree. With Mr. Williams's boys, it was always a risk to trust the words coming out their mouths. Mr. Williams treated them badly because they were his wife's from another man.

But my mom still needed the plums picked. So she told the boys to clean the tree and she'd split the basket with them.

We'd thought that was the end of that. Even when the dogs started up barking again farther into the gardens.

Then, all of the sudden, we heard something screaming, loud and shrill, like a child. Only it wasn't a child at all, it was the goat.

I grabbed the cutlass off the wall again and ran as fast as I could past the plum tree, the guava and baobab trees next to my grandfather's grave, through the bush, and into the gardens. The day was hot already, but I was too focused on the screaming goat and the feel of the machete's wooden handle in the grip of my right hand to notice. And then I was right on top of them: the dogs, mixed with pit for protection, their jaws locking onto the hind quarters of Mr. Williams's small goat, which was tied to a tree with a rope from some drug smuggler's boat found, perhaps, in the cove at Sommerset.

I couldn't think through all the screaming, the goat's sounding more human still than even the boys' behind me, and my mom's. I had a machete. They kept telling me to cut it loose, but I couldn't get around the dogs, tearing, tearing into flesh. It was then I noticed the heat, there with us all in the humid, tangled, buggy bush. I tried to slap the dogs away with the machete, until I realized you don't slap anything with a giant knife unless you're trying to kill it. Finally, I got to the rope. Cut it. And the goat took off into the estate, the dogs behind it; Rascal's jaw still locked on its left hind leg. The screaming continued for some time. And the dogs came home later, bloody, bloody.

My grandmother had to pay Mr. Williams the price of his goat, because Sommerset had been pivotal to my Uncle George's political party, had helped bring it into striking range. But later we heard rumors that maybe the goat hadn't died after all and that Mr. Williams had been able to heal its leg with salt water.

Her son not even cold in his grave and already Mama is starting this up again, telling Lil I can't be trusted with Godwyn because of that damn man and his goat. Saying she's to add Charles and Martin to the title.

What is Granny starting up again?

This business with the title to Godwyn—adding my brothers so neither of us can claim it.

Neither of "us" . . . So it's not about the goat.

No, Jean. It's not about the goat. You know damn well what it's about. And you have to fix it. You have to undo what you've done.

My lungs leaked their air.

It was my mom and Granny on the deed to Godwyn: survivor take all. Adding my uncles to inherit Granny's portion—my cousins would run my mom out in no time flat.

You should have kept your business to yourself, she goaded.

I tried. Still trying to remain calm.

You tried? Please, Jean. What kind of fool do you take me for? Mr. Henry lived his whole life in Baobique, led your uncle's constituency at Port Commons. You think his wife and children don't know about him carrying on with that man, that Trinidadian chef in Bato? You take us all for fools. But you're the fool, Jean. Look at what you've cost us.

Jesus, Mom. You think I meant for it to happen? Uncle Martin snuck up on us!

I don't need to hear the details! Just tell Granny you take it all back.

Take it all back? How?

Breath moving shallow and fast, shallow and fast, in and out of my lungs. I scanned my studio for somewhere to go. On the couch, my mother's many bags. She hadn't come to just rest for three weeks with the free plane ticket from my credit card company. She'd come to stay, to make her problem mine, until I took care of it.

I turned around, briefcase and house keys still in my hand from my arrival minutes earlier when I walked in on her and Auntie Lillian talking about me long distance, accruing some out-rageous phone bill I'd have to pay, and I walked back out the door.

Don't you walk out on me, young lady.

So I ran. I ran back out to the trendy street at the corner, down the block of restaurants, gourmet grocers, and upscale pet stores, ducked into the smallest coffee shop available, ordered a latte for comfort and disguise, should anyone wonder why I was there, in work clothes, in the middle of the day.

I knew my mom wouldn't wander that far. She always stayed close to home.

Chapter 7

WHEN UNCLE GEORGE'S TUMORS took a turn for the worse, I boarded a plane in San Francisco and for sixteen straight hours remembered why it was I didn't visit Baobique more often.

I flew American. American is the only major carrier that flies to the island of Baobique, in the West Indies. One night, in late October, from 10:00 in the evening until 2:00 the next afternoon, I flew on American airplanes, ran through American terminals, wrote in my American notebook printed in Roaring Springs, Pennsylvania, the state in which I attended college, to get from San Francisco to the very un-American island of Baobique, where I hoped to be able to say goodbye to my Uncle George before he died.

The tumor he'd gone to Canada to shrink had grown back, as anticipated. I'd talked with him the day before, the day everyone on my mother's side of the family started saying, *If you're going to visit, visit now.*

And so I flew all night, carried a week's needs on my back, held my breath until I could let him know I wanted to see him alive more than I wanted to be one of those people who'd maybe make it out for the funeral.

* * *

When I was eight, the year of my country's bicentennial, 1976, I visited Baobique with my mother for the first time. She cut my long hair short, short, taking a dull scissors to my head as I sat cross-legged at the kitchen table. She said it was too hot in Baobique, said I would overheat. But I knew she just didn't want to be bothered with the burden of braiding my hair when she returned home. The job I did on my own in the mornings was good enough for my country, but not for hers.

After my haircut, the first thing I did was run to the grocery store for some Lipton tea and low-fat milk. I was halfway down the first aisle when an old lady stopped me, took my round brown face in her blanched white hand, and announced to the entire produce section what an adorable little boy I was.

My Uncle George was the reason I became a lawyer. It was a reaction of sorts, a statement of purpose: to stand for that which he did not.

The last time I'd seen him, I had just graduated from college. I didn't know what I was going to do with my life, had liked political theory a lot. And at the time, Uncle George was Chief Minister of Baobique. I asked him if he could get me a job with the government for the summer, and he opened his home to me for as long as I wished.

That was the plan, anyway.

That whole summer, age twenty-two, I ran every morning. I was the only jogger in Baobique. To this day, there is still only one paved road that circles the island, a second that cuts through the interior at the mid-point. I'd run up the interior road, up past the construction workers who, because of my short, short hair and boyish build, would yell out, *Man or 'oman? Man or 'oman?* just after I crossed into view. Sending themselves into hysterics. I'd run up to the thin waterfall pouring out the side of the cliff, just past the little river where I saw for the first time that sideways-running hermit crab, looking like it was heading away from what it wanted, or maybe moving straight toward it and only seeming sideways. Sometimes I'd run all the way to the Hughes Estate, a bed-and-breakfast now, but once a big banana plantation.

I also walked a lot. Once, I walked all the way to Milieu, down the stretch of road called One-Mile, where my grandmother still owned fifty or sixty acres. It was a Wednesday and I saw the banana trucks headed past me to the port in Bato. But just past the orchid farm run by a couple of Canadians, my uncle's law partner, Gerald, stopped me, turned me back, told me I'd *better not wander so far from home.*

Gerald must have said something to Uncle George, because soon after that my uncle came home early from work, put me in his 1970 Toyota, its right-side drive, drove me around the entire island. An escort. From the car, the narrowness of that single road made the cliffs that dropped from its sides and the forests that crept over its top feel close, close.

We started out on the De Canne side of the closest mountain to the Bato coast. I had been jogging it daily and I knew each turn of the road on a more intimate level than my uncle assumed. Yet each of those turns, each stretch of new pavement, attached to some part of his life; the road itself, one of his recent accomplishments, was the product of a fruitful negotiation with the Japanese government.

We drove until we reached the Carib Reserve, a small area deemed to have symbolic importance now that there are so few Caribs left on the island. The Caribs came up from South America and killed off all of the original inhabitants of Baobique, the Arawaks. The Caribs were then almost completely killed off by or mixed in with those who came next, the Europeans and their imported African slaves. They are brown-skinned, with straight black hair and flat noses. They were extremely fierce before the Europeans came. Now they weave beautiful handicrafts for the tourists and a couple of them have very nice one-room hotels. My uncle and I stopped at one for a drink.

After we left the Carib Reserve, Uncle George pointed to an outcrop just before we reached Tete Queue, upon which stood an old house; he said that was where an American homosexual used to live, a man he had run off the island for corrupting the local boys with his disgusting practices.

At twenty-two, I didn't know much, didn't know what my future held in store. But my hands sunk underneath my legs as I sat in Uncle George's passenger seat, fingers trembling, knowing I was one of those Americans my uncle would never voluntarily welcome into his home, drive around his island, or kiss goodnight. I also knew I was scared. I was scared for him to know. So I called the airline that night. Told them I needed to leave Baobique. Bought myself a three-legged ticket to California: Baobique to San Juan, San Juan to Houston, Houston to San Francisco, on American for safety. My future path turned out to be a silent statement of protest. I never could bring myself to be myself in his presence.

Cynthia told me she knew at twelve. Coming back from summer camp and her first kiss from another girl, her mother finding a love note folded into a square, stuck in with the laundry, and promptly sending Cynthia into therapy to get it, whatever it was, reversed. My first lover knew at fourteen, when she had her first affair, with a twenty-six-year-old female drummer in a local band, spending the next six years drunk, sober at twenty.

I only admitted I was gay at twenty-two, to myself, sitting in the passenger seat of my Uncle George's Toyota, as he told me, through the story of a homosexual he ran off the island, that gay Americans were not safe in Baobique while he was around. He'd gone on to tell me he didn't stop there, that he'd since established and enforced some of the strictest anti-sodomy laws in the Caribbean, with criminal penalties of five to ten years in prison for the touching of the wrong peoples' privates. The kind of laws that make Americans call places like Baobique backward.

Before I fled his island, I sat with him in his living room while he hosted a white Californian eco-tourist that one of my cousins brought by. The tourist didn't know he was talking to the Chief Minister, and proceeded, as many do, to tell my uncle exactly how his country should be run. I was embarrassed, disgusted by the tourist and any of him I might have inside me for also being an American, relishing the moment my cousin explained to the mortified tourist who my uncle was like I have relished few others in my life.

Still, my plan was to steal some of his power. If he was there to make laws that made people like me illegal, I'd be somewhere else fighting back.

Problem was he'd scared me, and I wanted his love too much.

When I left my uncle's house that trip, running back to my United States so the part of me that was gay could think straight, I left behind the part that was Baobiquen, as if removing one layer of myself to save another. It was as if I was choosing sides without knowing it, as if I was taking sides against myself.

I went to law school in San Francisco, where I felt safe. And I practiced civil rights beyond his reach.

Civil rights? They don't need civil rights in San Francisco. They have too many already, he'd tease on the phone. But I knew he was proud of me for following him into law. Trusting him with my life's choices, like that.

I hadn't the courage to go back for nearly a decade. And only then because Uncle George was dying. It was he, it seemed, who kept me coming and going, coming and going.

When Uncle George found out he had brain cancer, my Uncle Charles, a doctor in Canada, made him fly up to North America for chemotherapy. Baobique's medical advancements have been few. Its hospital, understaffed and overcrowded, had started using wooden pallets for beds, lining them up on the floor in rows.

So Uncle George went to Canada to have his tumor shrunk. And in the cold, colorless land of modern medicine, Uncle George shrank right along with it. When he talked at all, he talked of rowing his dingy in the sea for exercise. Eventually, he told his brother that when the next round of chemotherapy was finished, he was going back home, to Baobique. He knew the tumor would come back. The day before I flew to see him, its bulk pressed up against the part of his brain that controlled his right side, paralyzing his leg, his arm, and half his face, so he slurred his words a bit when we spoke on the phone and he asked *when* I was coming. They later called it, the resultant paralysis, a *mass effect*.

Before I landed in Baobique to see him, Beckford Hall being heavily trafficked for the funeral of the late Prime Minister, my plane circled the island twice. And from the air Baobique looked, as it always does, newly sprouted out of the seas—on one side the Atlantic, on the other the Caribbean—a solid mass of green sticking straight up and held there by the top of a volcano anchored deep below, like a gigantic Chia pet, dark green, combed back by winds coming, maybe, all the way from Africa, continuing, maybe, all the way to San Francisco.

I had never seen so many cars at Beckford Hall. They spilled over the small lot and onto the tarmac. Dignitaries from our plane and others right behind would be driven into Bato, the capital, for the weekend. They would pass the Hill Estate on the way, the family home of the late Prime Minister, the Socialist, who would be buried there against his wishes.

At customs, a victory of sorts. The young officer didn't check my overstuffed backpack after I told him I was on island to visit my sick uncle, George Pascal, and was staying with my mom, his sister, at Godwyn. A victory of sorts, because I had no explanation for the five electronic rodent traps my mom had asked me to bring.

My mom and Auntie Clara picked me up in the jeep. On the way to Tours, both of them at once, explaining something to me.

Tours is my grandmother's house, built for her by my grand-father after their children had all grown and left the family home at Godwyn. It is more yard than house, the house more functional than beautiful. To look at, it is not much; it is not pretty like my mom's Godwyn, or Uncle George's house in De Canne with his wall of windows looking out onto the sea.

Tours is simple: cement blocks painted white on the outside, off-white on the inside; one story, three bedrooms spun off a central dining and living area; kitchen in back. My grandmother, after the big hurricane in the '70s, walled in half the front porch with more of the cinder blocks, unpainted, meant to let air through but not much light. The other half she secured with wrought iron bars, painted brown. The porch is where we gathered, mostly because that is where my grandmother could always be found, on her lawn chair, staring outside through the bars.

Only recently had Granny conceded to allow piped-in water, the rainwater basin on the roof always providing enough for her. Out front she just sat and stared, ignoring everyone until she needed some tea, or toast, or to explain to someone exactly how what they were doing was completely wrong, staring all the while off Tours' cliff, at its cove and the gentle Caribbean. At night, the moon.

As my mom and Auntie Clara drove me home from the airport, away from the throng of dignitaries in for the Hill funeral,

Granny was waiting for us, expecting us to stay at least a night or two before even stopping by Godwyn to drop off our bags or for my mom to check on her dogs and their new puppies.

The jeep took us right up to Granny's front porch, where she was sitting in her lawn chair; Uncle George, also sitting, in a similar chair at his mother's side, propped up by pillows and blankets, wearing a powder-blue polo shirt. He smiled at me, and half his face remained stationary from the mass effect earlier that week, after which he didn't get medical treatment for two days; his doctor, we realized, was just waiting for him to die. Uncle George did not comply. Granny hired a new physician. Later, as the paralysis lessened a bit, Uncle George entertained us with jokes about the fired doctor, his favorite, seemingly: *Dr. Munce is a dunce.*

Although he was sitting up when I arrived, he had not gotten there by himself and was not able to stay there long. Mostly, he had to lie down, being turned from side to side every few hours to keep the blood flowing. Mostly, he snored, whether awake or asleep, because his larynx was paralyzed and he couldn't clear the mucus properly from the back of his throat.

Chapter 8

O N PIEDMONT AVENUE, I sat and stared out the window of the coffee shop at the yuppie women with babies, women whose husbands were at work. Every now and then, a stay-at-home dad.

I started thinking thoughts I'm ashamed to own, like how much easier my life would be if I were straight. Sitting there in the coffee shop, cold hands curled around my latte as I hid from my mother, it was clear I wasn't. It had been nearly a year since I'd last seen Susan. Yet my body remembered immediately. My tongue against hers as we kissed and I protested the rain, she assuring me it wasn't raining, it was *just the sun washing himself.* My fingers warming to the touch of the mug.

My fingers remembered. They remembered their trembling, shaky glide up and down the slick opening between her legs; the sides of her soft like the lips covering her mouth. My fingers remembered her tongue; they remembered its trembling, shaky glide up and down the inside of my palm. They remembered pushing inside her; remembered her warm and closing in, closing out the footsteps coming up from behind, until it was too late, the voices, the din of my family. They remembered, my fingers, the rhythms to which she responded, the rhythms that matched her breaths the closer she got, the louder she got, giving us away; my fingers remembered their rhythm inside her, they remembered her breath matching their pulse.

It was Susan's sounds that masked their footsteps, at first her breath coming quicker and quicker, her short cries, and finally, her low moan.

We had gone as far away from the house, as far into the gardens at Godwyn, as possible. Not out in the open, under the neon of the Flamboyant tree. Bright orange. We'd sought somewhere muted. Through the bush to the far end of the estate. Next to the cliff, its rocks and steep drop. Underneath a baobab. Above the constant shifting of the gray-black waves just before the storm coming in, we took turns leading each other there.

It was Uncle Martin who found us, followed us is more like it. He and Mr. Williams. They'd waited. Watched. Susan's shaky touch, fingers first, circling curls at the back of my neck; her increasingly confident bottom lip; teeth—pulling skin. And when they'd had their fill, they started up with their indignant shouts. *Jesus Christ, girls! This is no way for you two to get along. Get up out of the dirt. Get up this instant!*

Mr. Williams's eyes just about to pop out of their sockets. Their jaws on the ground. Both men bulging, big as bananas, in their pants.

Susan was a Hill. Unless one of those letters that had finally stopped coming to me in Oakland carried an unwritten announcement and her family had managed to marry her off— or some other such nonsense. She'd been a resident physician on one of the Virgin Islands, come home for the funeral of her uncle. Baobique is such a small place, everyone is someone. My first time back in ten years, since I was scared away after college by Uncle George and his strong feelings against gay Americans. She'd been on my plane from San Juan. I remembered her green eyes against her coffee-brown skin and, as it turned out, she, mine.

Susan stopped by to check in on Uncle George after hearing about his mass effect when everyone was still calling it a stroke. She was the one to correct us, explained to my family that his paralysis was due to the swelling of the tumor pressing against parts of his brain, inhibiting voluntary movement.

She stopped by Tours my second morning, I was helping in the kitchen.

The novelty of my arrival had worn off and I had become simply one of the team of women that worked to keep Uncle George fed, dry, and away from any possibility of slipping into a depression.

Nights were heavy work, literally, when the need for sandwiches and juice temporarily gave way to carrying Uncle George to the toilet two or three times, in the dark. The first night of the paralysis, before Uncle Charles arrived, Uncle Martin got stuck in Bato, leaving only my mom, Auntie Clara, and Granny at the house; Granny in her thin cotton nightshirt worn nearly through from the years, barking directions from her bed across the dining room. Mom and Auntie Clara able to move their brother—his entire left side dead weight—to the bathroom and onto the commode, but unable, for hours after, to move him back. Uncle George, all the while, sitting soiled and naked, pulling into sadness. It took the arrival of Uncle Charles and me, both flying in from North America, to get him into a clean shirt and out next to Granny on the porch, joking about his negligent physician, saying things like, *Dr. Munce is a dunce,* through heavy, heavy lips.

Not one to support the usual division of labor by gender at Tours, but not being strong enough to help lift my increasingly small uncle even to arrange his pillows, during the day I did whatever I could for the men who'd had night duty.

I am normally considered a relatively capable person, not one to shy away from things that require a little grit. But my relatives are not privy to my capable side and, admittedly, I do not shine in a kitchen.

I was raised in suburban Illinois and for the last fifteen years or so have lived in Northern California, the populated parts, mostly urban. I have always lived in places where, if I wanted fresh juice, I could pick it up at the corner store. Likewise, my fish and chicken always came to me pre-packaged, scaled, plucked, and unbloody. Additionally, I rarely have to cook for ten or twelve people at a time.

The first obstacle I encountered that morning, during my attempt at preparing a lunch of ham sandwiches for the ten of us, was a dull carving knife, a knife I had to share with Valerie, my grandmother's maid, as she chopped the chicken for dinner. The bread, thank God, was pre-sliced. There was mayonnaise and mustard, Dijon, in the fridge. The ham itself, my second obstacle, a giant thigh of pig, and I was a vegetarian. The fridge at Tours was probably older than I was and had decided to be weak along with Uncle George. Its main section wasn't cold enough to keep the meat from going bad overnight, so the ham had been put in the freezer. It was frozen. Solid. There was nothing else for lunch. My healthy uncles had been up all night carrying their brother's body to and from the toilet, cleaning his soiled skin and night clothes as they laughed with him about almost anything they could think of, so he wouldn't feel sad, or humiliated. And I, in the kitchen in the middle of the day, couldn't figure out how to make a ham sandwich. I got them coffee to hold them over, that alone taking me thirty minutes because I had to share the outlet with Valerie.

I'll just eat bread and mayonnaise if it takes much longer, Jean, said Uncle Charles, the physician from Canada, who suggested only then that I employ the microwave under the towel in the corner to defrost the meat once the electric socket was free.

I was able, with the dull knife I told Valerie she could not have back until I finished the sandwiches, to hack off chunks of pig thigh and heat out the ice in the microwave. I had no trouble at all with the microwave, thank you very much. Two by two, I got them sandwiches. The men went first because they were up all night. Susan second, because she was a guest. Then Granny. Then my aunts. It took me an hour and a half. But I had succeeded in giving Uncle George something else to laugh about. And I had succeeded in making a friend of Susan.

Later, I sat on Uncle George's good side. He asked me whether I thought he was ready to walk as yet. I told him, maybe soon, maybe just then it was a little too ambitious.

What evidence do you have for that statement? asked the barrister.

Well, none. It was a political statement, rather than one based on evidence. I was just trying to make everyone happy.

And I'd succeeded. Smiling back, he reminded me, *You are talking to someone who has been an excellent politician.* As he sipped the grapefruit juice I squeezed and strained special for him out of his spill-proof children's cup, Uncle George told me it was the *best juice* he'd ever had, and thanked me. He said I would make someone a wonderful wife some day. I was not to listen to the others.

Susan returned several hours later. We piled into Uncle Martin's Four-Runner at a quarter past 6:00, just the five of us: Susan, my mom, Uncle Charles, Uncle Martin, and myself. Still time for a quick sea bath before dark, Tours Beach so close, its red clay path just across the street and down a couple hundred feet from Granny's.

Uncle Martin climbed into the driver's seat wearing slacks, said he'd swim in his briefs. It would give the women a much-awaited chance to laugh at him, he said. A pleasure far exceeding any embarrassment he could possibly experience.

He was joking. A trial lawyer, Uncle Martin had long been untroubled by personal feelings of embarrassment, his daily sub-jugation to the wrath and ridicule of judges having dulled the most unnecessary layers of his self-respect, leaving him with only those closest to the nerve.

Martin! Don't drive through Mama's garden! Uncle Martin drove out Granny's yard, crossing against some imaginary bound-ary between driveway and garden Granny thought proper, but which was really just a big space, plenty wide enough for a truck to drive through and leave no trace of its passage.

On the street, tall palms blocked our view of the ocean, part-ing magically at the entrance to the road that led to the family beach. Uncle Martin let out a war cry. Shifted down.

The ruts in the clay road swallowed the tires halfway, rain water splashing out of them as we plunged forward. *You have to keep moving not to get stuck in the holes.*

To tarish the road with gravel would have made the beach too accessible to others, who would certainly damage this family tra-dition, Tours Beach, if invited by the paving. But Uncle Martin had already dug the drainage paths along each side, so when the time came, he could pave the road in a single day by bringing in the tarish at dawn. They would only pave this road when they developed the area for tourists.

Uncle Martin had recently sold a portion of the family's land—to pay off some of Uncle George's mounting medical bills—to the Socialist government, just before Archibald Hill, Susan's uncle, passed away. The government promptly discovered a rich tarish reserve on the property and began a multi-million-dollar excavating operation to benefit the people of Baobique. But no sense in second guessing one's self. When the time had come to make the decision, Uncle Martin had made it. He had pulled the family out of a hole and was satisfied with that.

Grampy used to say a good sea bath would heal any wound. But Granny was frightened of our going to the beach, because some squatters had threatened to chop us up into tiny bits if we went there after Uncle Martin had the police tear down their thatched leaf shelters. The squatters had tried to reason; they told Uncle Martin, if he made them leave, they'd tell everyone he was not a nice man. My uncle was perplexed, asked them, *Why would I want anyone to think I was a nice man?!*

When we reached the water, Uncle Martin and Uncle Charles stripped: Uncle Martin down to his briefs; Uncle Charles, prepared, to his Speedo. We entered with varying degrees of tolerance. Uncle Martin's briefs turned translucent and we all began to float. On our backs in the warm sea, eyes on the changing shades of blue as the sun receded from the rest of our day, a few half-erased clouds here and there, Uncle Martin explained things to us. He explained that the dark areas in the water were schools of small silverfish, good to eat but hard to catch enough for a meal. When the moon was right, whenever that was, people came down with white sheets and scooped the silverfish up by the sheetfull and they twinkled like stars in the night. He explained why it was necessary to send his brother, Uncle George, to Martinique one last time for an MRI, to check the progression of his tumors. Certain family members could then be shown the true extent of the cancer, begin to let go of their denial. He explained that George's law practice, the best on the island, was in jeopardy of being out-balanced by the other partner's family, since Gerald's son had just joined the firm. He explained it would only take a year or two for me, already an attorney under the U.S. system, to gain my license in the West Indies and promised me, if I worked hard, a respectable living should I ever choose to move to Baobique. I should think about it. Consider it.

Shifting, Uncle Martin explained to us the difficulties he was having with his wife, how his desire to slow down his work pace was incompatible with her desire for more and more money. He explained to us we should *never marry a woman*, grinning widely at his joke, explaining to my shocked mother that *woman* and *man* are the same thing in law.

He looked over at us, annoyed. Susan and I engaged in easy conversation, half-listening to him to be polite, attention fixed on each other instead.

Just then a school of the small fish swam directly into my floating body, dozens upon dozens jumping out of the sea, onto my chest, my face, my flailing arms as I tried to move. Elevated tone, Uncle Martin explained that we should move away quickly. It meant the silverfish were being chased by a bigger one.

Lessons learned, we drove home in the warm breeze of the growing darkness. My hands sunk underneath my legs in the passenger seat, fingers trembling and my breath coming shallow and fast, shallow and fast.

Dinner, I took out to the porch, sat in my grandmother's chair, and stared at her moon.

Chapter 9

UNCLE MARTIN WAS ALWAYS LOOKING to be someone more important than the man he really was: always in the shadow of Uncle George. One of Baobique's lesser mountains.

He won his chance when he and Mr. Williams followed us into the gardens at Godwyn, through the bush to the far end of the estate, watched Susan and me pull each other close.

And he ran with it, ran us all the way back to Tours, just as Mr. Williams ran down to Sommerset. Both men bursting with the news—*a Hill and a Pascal, two women, caught in the dirt, acting like one a dem shoulda been a man. I tell you, it was a SIGHT to see.* Neither man believing the luck he'd unearthed out there just past Grampy's grave.

At Tours, it was decided. Uncle Martin and Uncle Charles discussed the settlement over a bottle of rum around the dining table, as Susan and I sat, prey to a movement we couldn't control, at either end. My mom and Auntie Clara busying themselves making sardine sandwiches in the kitchen, and Granny listening from her lawn chair on the front porch, the sea blast carrying their angry voices and our silence straight to her ears on pregnant beads of moisture.

Uncle Charles did the speaking.

He screamed. *Five years in prison, Jean! Five years! This isn't San Francisco, woman. What filth have you brought here?*

Dirt and clay caked to the back of both my elbows, eyes to the floor, all I could see was my own shame—stripped and naked with nowhere to hide.

How could you do this to us? How could you do this to George? Are you trying to kill him?

Uncle Martin chimed in, *Do you know what will happen if Mr. Williams tells the local police? They'll lock you up for gross indecency. And what could we say, na? George wrote the law himself!*

Uncle Charles: *You'd put that choice to him? You'd make your dying uncle lock up his favorite niece for this?*

Susan and I sat silent at the dining table, its white cloth glowing in the coming of the dark.

The women were silent: Granny on her porch, Auntie Clara in the kitchen, my mom in the doorway just watching.

This was men's work. If Susan and I had been men ourselves, we'd have been facing ten years, not five.

Looking back, I see how much danger we were really in. I didn't have to be scared all those years I'd stayed away from Baobique, but I'd been wise to keep my mouth shut about being gay.

No one is out in Baobique. They can't be.

Susan and I were never to see each other again. My uncles said since neither of us lived on the island, and I rarely even visited, they would be able to laugh off the rumors certain to spread from Sommerset. They would simply deny it ever happened.

From his bedroom, Uncle George overheard the whole thing. He didn't have to be dead to roll over in his grave, turn his slouching back to me. The next morning, the morning of the Hill funeral, bright and early, he had Uncle Charles give him a shave, a proper shave with his straight-edged razor from London. And just as Granny began working herself up over company expected after the funeral, Uncle George called me over to his good side. I fed him a sip of grapefruit juice I had just squeezed in the kitchen to keep myself from the vulnerability of idleness.

Very slowly, through heavy, heavy lips, Uncle, the orator, took me into his confidence: *There is something about an island, Jean. It gets in your blood. I could have stayed in Canada for treatment. I would have lived longer. But there are worse things than death, to me.*

His breathing was even, from the depth of his lungs. Calm.

When the people in Sommerset had only the river and rain water to wash their clothes and supply their houses, I put in two water spouts, one at either end of the village. So they had running water close by. And when they started using those spouts every day, and the road became muddy from the spills, and the red mud caked on the old women's feet as they carried their jugs back and forth to their homes, I paved that road so it would be easier for them to access the water.

That simple thing, a water spout, won me the constituency. It made them feel someone cared, made them feel they were as important as the people in Bato, or Port Commons. And that one village gave us our green light for the coup. You see, nothing is too small to be over-looked. In politics, the tiniest village can take on a significance far greater than its actual size.

Until that water spout—no, until I paved that road—I was get-ting rotten tomatoes thrown at me during my campaign speeches. Rotten tomatoes. This scar above my eyebrow, from a rock.

The pull of his breath took on a labored air but didn't stop him. His breathing more and more audible.

Do you know that most Baobiquens have two telephones at home? Two telephones. One CarCom and one Cable and Wireless. The CarCom telephone plan is much cheaper. But there is a catch. The CarCom telephone is only compatible with other CarCom phones. Both parties must be on CarCom to communicate. If I call you on

CarCom, you must receive my call on your CarCom phone. So, to use CarCom, you must know beforehand that the recipient has CarCom. Same telephone number as the Cable and Wireless phone. Same ring.

Most Baobiquens—not all, but most—have CarCom. We must always try CarCom first for local calls because it is a Baobiquen company, locally owned. While the Cable and Wireless devices can accommodate both local and long distance calls, Cable and Wireless is a British company and none of their revenue benefits us.

Sometimes, for a joke, we answer our telephones by saying: CarCom to CarCom. *But I tell you, it is no joke. It is survival.*

He had some trouble with the saliva collecting at the base of his lazy larynx. Yet Uncle George pushed on, cleared his throat with force. Focused.

You would be surprised at the extent to which your First World countries try to take advantage of our little island. They are most shameless. We must continually resist their exploitation.

Years ago, when you were a child, just about the same time your country celebrated their bicentennial anniversary of independence, Baobique celebrated its first. We were no longer a British commonwealth. But it is not easy for such a small island to be self-sufficient, so when the formation of the European Union took away our major source of income and the United Kingdom stopped subsidizing our banana exports, we could no longer remain hidden from the rest of the world. If we did not reach out and develop new contracts, we would not survive. Instead of telling your big corporations to take their business elsewhere, we welcomed them.

But we have done, I believe, a commendable job of resisting temptation and limiting foreign ownership on the island. We do not want to go the way of Antigua, its land stripped of all but its white sand beaches; an entire population watched bloodshot by fraternity boys through the bottoms of beer mugs on their spring holiday. What do you call it? Spring break.

Uncle George's breathing grew as loud as his voice.

You would be surprised at how difficult it is to steer a different course for Baobique. It is a constant battle. Constant. With the wrong leadership, a few thoughtless decisions, it would not take long to lose all this, to turn our rain forests, our valleys, our mountains, into a First World playground, to be unwrapped, used up, and discarded by American tourists. And then what would we Baobiquens be left with? Answer me that.

And so we have fought to keep out companies who offer us U.S. dollars at the expense of long-term sustainability. When your Caribou Cruise Lines wanted to come into Bato seven days a week, monopolize our only deep-water harbor at the expense of all other exports, so that hundreds of tourists could pour into our capital every day, litter our streets, over-use our trails to places like Soufre Lake and Victoria Falls, cut through our rain forests for better access—when the cruise line tried to do that, we just smiled. When it came time to negotiate their contract, again we smiled, but we told them they'd have to pay the Baobiquen workers who would clean their toilets, cook their caliloo and fried plantain, the same wages they paid their American employees.

Of course, we knew they wouldn't. They offered to build us a second deep-water port, up near Granny, in De Cote, just so they could keep the tourists streaming in. But the long-term costs to the island would have been detrimental.

Our constituents in Bato were not happy they did not get those new jobs and they did not get that regular supply of fresh tourists to put shoes on their children's feet. Explaining the breakdown in the contract negotiations with the cruise line to the public was a delicate maneuver. In the end, it worked best to create a diversion. To take their minds off that problem. Give them something else to worry about . . . There are some times, Jean, when creativity is a government official's most important asset. And, I tell you, they do not teach you that in law school.

There were countless victories in the work.

My uncle paused to regain the composure pilfered by his paralysis, his breath slow and steady, returning to him like an obedient dog to its master after only a few seconds.

I've told you about the American fellow, in Tete Queue, who came to the island and took up living there. The homosexual who began, shall we say, corrupting *some of the local boys. Do you know what he would do, Jean? Do you? He'd call them in for cold juice or rum, or some other such pretense, and they'd wind up doing only God knows what unspeakable things. So when he tried to buy a house on the island, to live here permanently, he ran into his share of bureaucratic obstacles: land surveys not using the right valuation formula, missing signatures, unexpected deadlines. I made sure of that.*

And I'm certainly not saying this is true, but I also heard rumors that some of my constituents in Tete Queue approached him about leaving the island late one night when the generator supplying the area with its electricity wasn't running and the moon was just a sliver in the sky.

He left quite abruptly. American Airlines flight 2330.

Uncle George had hit his stride, spoke clearly even through the slack in his face.

These are the moral victories that made my political work most satisfying. Because—listen closely, Jean, you must not forget this—just as we must preserve Baobiquen culture by resisting the economic exploitation that will scavenge the best from our island for the whimsy of American tourists and leave us destitute in twenty years time; just as we must choose the services of our local companies, like CarCom, before we succumb to the convenience of First World corporations— just as important to the health of our island is its moral cleanliness. We cannot have people like that here in Baobique.

I admit my law practice has suffered since I entered politics. At times, your Uncle Martin has had to take on some of my overflow cases. But the truth is, the work I most enjoyed was never the litigation. The work I most enjoyed was the politics.

When I served as Chief Minister, under Prime Minister Devon, Dame Devon, for the Liberty Party, I effected more change on this island than a hundred lawsuits.

When I ask myself, Jean, if I have lived a good life, it is not just me who answers. It is also the old women in Sommerset with running water; it is those boys in Tete Queue who will grow to have wives and children; it is their parents; it is the collective voice of Baobique.

Ask yourself that question in twenty years time. And see what you have to say for yourself.

Thank you for coming, Jean. But it is time for you to leave Baobique.

Chapter 10

AT MY TABLE IN THE COFFEE SHOP, I had forgotten to drink my latte. My fingers, turned cold as milk, curled tight around the circle of the mug and heavy with the weight of remembering, felt for the envelope in the outside pocket of my briefcase. Thin, blue airmail stationery worn thinner from handling. Mine.

I already knew each line, what it asked that never got answered. I opened it up, even though I didn't need to, skipped to the same part I always did, like a broken record since I'd received it, months before:

They do not read the mail here, you know, like they do at the Post Office in Bato. So if that is what is stopping you from writing, it shouldn't.

My residency in Nassau will end in six months. I have options, J. There are fellowships in California well within my reach. But they are of no interest to me without a reason to be that far from home. And you would be the best judge of that. You need to tell me if I have a reason. If you want me, you have to say so.

I can come to the States. But this is not a decision I will make without you. It is hard for me to believe that you've yet to respond to any of my letters. You are not alone, J. I am also confused. But I know we both felt a certainty in Baobique. And I cannot get that back by myself. Tell me, how on God's green earth can you hide from me? Even now, I see you. I know you better than you know yourself, Pascal. You are so damn difficult.

I would never force a decision on you. But I am telling you, now, I will not wait forever. You are making a mistake.

I would like to believe that love feels better than this. I would like for you to be the one to convince me of that.

The meanest thing I ever did was never write her back; never tell Susan that if we were in the second grade I'd have picked her for my best, best friend, told her everything in my whole world, like who was cuter, Mark or Brennen, candy bars just went up to twenty-six cents, and how to cross the monkey bars two by two. But I am not in the second grade anymore, and wanting her that much got all complicated and threatening. And so I tripped. Left us both to land on our own.

There are things I've done I can't forgive. I know what it is to disregard an outstretched hand.

A fog had settled along the trendy street, unusual for early afternoon, obscuring visibility. I bussed my table of its still-full mug, readied myself to leave the coffee shop, leaned against the glass door, taking three tries to push it open, and retraced my earlier frantic flight, diffuse in the blue-gray mist.

Making sure to make noise as I climbed the steps, I opened the door braced for the chill of my mother's reproach. But she wasn't there, the only things staring back at me, my four bare walls and all her bags.

At 10 o'clock I called the Oakland Police. My mom, missing only eight hours, was not a priority for them, but they did, after half an hour on hold, take my report over the phone. They told me to look in places familiar. And to check the local hospitals.

But I didn't move. I didn't make any other calls. I sat in the center of my futon, wedged between two of her too many bags, stared out the window, and waited.

That, I knew how to do: wait. The day my sick uncle looked me in the eye and asked me to leave his island—disgraced that I'd been caught with Susan—I did as I was told. I kissed both his cheeks, drove back to Godwyn, a passenger in my mother's jeep on an unfamiliar side of the street, and packed my backpack. I hadn't needed the black mourning clothes, after all.

And then I waited. I sat on my mother's bed, stared out her open window, out past Grampy's grave, the spreading baobab, the steep drop to the bottomless ocean—Baobique nothing more than an ancient volcano, raised to the surface of the water from depths unimaginable.

I sat there for hours, until Rascal and Lucia started raising a ruckus underneath the window. The intrusion of their barking more than I could bear, I got up to shush them. And when I moved to the window, Susan was there; the mixture of our smells, still on my skin that day. The dogs had allowed her cautious access.

She reached up her hands to meet me halfway, slowed my drop as I climbed out my mother's window.

We matched each other step for step. And held on, out back, for all the ghosts to see, until the sun dropped below the horizon, took its final rest.

This is not the way we will end, Jean. It isn't a forever goodbye, just a temporary one. She promised.

But the next afternoon I got on a plane, and for the next year, every time Susan took a step toward me, she took it alone.

* * *

The night sky never turns all the way black in Oakland like it does on my mother's island. In Baobique, when it's dark, it's just the same to have your eyes open as to have them shut. But in Oakland, the streetlights and the fog keep it white underneath— my mother missing that night, everything reflected back to me, making it impossible to throw a single thought away as I waited for her to return. Like playing handball against a brick wall, the ball just coming back faster the harder I swung.

The telephone rang me awake at dawn. A man with a gentle voice apologized for the hour of his call, hoped he had the right number, said to me, *I believe your mother just spent the night on my front porch.*

Where are you? Where do you live? Breath shallow and fast, shallow and fast.

I live in Redwood City, 245 Mira Vista. At—

The corner of Alta Mont.

How do you know? His gentle voice inching toward concern.

Is my mother all right!?

Well, she's having some tea. She told me you were her lawyer and gave me your business card. I don't think she's well. She thinks I've stolen her house. She's asked me to leave.

Oh God. I can be there in forty minutes . . . We used to live in your house. It was a long time ago . . . My mother is going through a rough time. I'm sorry. I'll be there as soon as I can.

Chapter 11

I PULLED ON MY JEANS, stumbled into my little gray Mazda, and raced to the freeway. Six-thirty Tuesday morning. Traffic was already clogging here and there across the bridge leaving Oakland, driving into San Francisco. The day had begun, whether I liked it or not. I took the 101, perhaps as punishment; its sound-resistant walls, their brick veneer, preventing, like the white of the night before, the escape of my thoughts. I was stuck with myself and the reverse-commuters leaving San Francisco, heading down the peninsula.

I would not, I admit, have been an easy child for my mother to raise alone after the divorce, often thinking myself, at twelve or thirteen, more capable than she at governing my life. Even when she had the strength to try, I resisted with all my might.

Once, on the 4th of July in junior high, Becky, my sometimes best friend, and I both made the All-Star softball team. We got to play under the big lights that night, stayed out on our bikes way past the end of the fireworks at the local commons, soft wind growing cooler as each hour deepened toward morning.

Becky lived just a few houses down, and when we got to our street, we could both see the cop car parked in front of my house. It was 2 o'clock in the morning.

My mom, scared something happened to me, had called the

police. I remember carrying my bike up the front steps, walking it through the screen door, wondering what we had for anyone to steal.

But what I remember most about that 4th of July was thinking, *Who's she* to be calling the law, playing parent, imposing punishment? Near as I could tell, she was always upstairs in bed, half-gallon jug of cheap white wine propped up by the stack of condensed classics that covered the half of the bed that used to be my father's, and would soon belong to Harold, her second boyfriend, the one I wouldn't have liked no matter what, the one who would throw me against the refrigerator for flipping him the bird, the one who would save her, or so she thought, from laying upstairs indefinitely. Near as I could tell, when my mom wasn't at work, selling men's clothes to our middle-class neighbors, on her feet for eight, nine, ten hours a day, she was at home in bed—hadn't taken notice of me in years.

Harold took my mother from Illinois to California; he took the money she made from the sale of our Victorian, peeling paint and exposed wood, its weathered façade so close to the Wright houses the new owners didn't care they'd have to repaint, the fairness of their skin alone restoring property values more than any coat of red or white.

They'd met in the men's department at Marshall Field's.

She'd sold him a gray wool suit just before closing and he'd seen her in the parking lot, offered her a ride home in his ultra-compact Honda Civic.

Six months later, she sold our house and Harold drove us across the country.

Harold was white, like my father. But unlike my father, he was American, which made all the difference. Harold had served in the Pacific during World War II—he was *that* old—my mother's brown skin reminding him, perhaps, of a time when it was acceptable to take open advantage of someone like her.

I would like to think my mother loved me more than she did Harold. But the truth is, I don't know. It took Harold to get her out of bed. Not me. I used to sit at the top of the stairs, just in front of her closed door, listening for signs of life until it was time to fix myself dinner or put myself to sleep.

It took Harold to move us from Illinois to California. Redwood City. Mira Vista at Alta Mont.

I used to hear them in the master bedroom, creaky bed springs, slapping skin, rhythmic cries of relief from my mother's lips as if he was pumping the life back into her that my father, years ago, and I, daily, drained out.

My mom put all the money from the sale of our house into Harold's, helping him lower the monthly mortgage payments by nearly a thousand dollars.

Of all the places Harold took my mom, and all the things he took from her, mostly he took her for granted. The only thing they ever did together was have sex and eat dinner: cubed steak, potatoes, and frozen vegetables in the middle of California.

After dinner he'd sneak into the garage, through the door that led down from the kitchen, where he hoarded day-old baked goods in greasy brown paper bags on top of a loose two-by-four in the ceiling; each night he'd eat stale jelly doughnuts by himself.

Those other things they did—creaky bed springs, breathy cries at night—I mostly heard from the other side of the wall. But through the keyhole I could see the little lump of them, single and pulsating: up and down, up and down.

Maybe I'm more like Uncle Martin than I'd like to admit, because my body responded. Breathy and imminent. Wet and taut. Maybe if I'd had a little banana between my legs, it would have been standing, straight to, right then, like his did watching Susan and me. Maybe sex just shames us; makes us angry at everyone involved.

The way Harold was made it easy for me to hate him: old, closed, and inflexible. It was easier than I could have imagined, sneaking into the garage, stealing his day-olds, feeding them to the squirrels underneath the persimmon tree in the backyard, leaving the greasy bags empty and balled up on the counter by the sliding-glass door so he'd be sure to see.

It was much easier than blocking out my mom. I remember clearly, deciding that night not to see her over there, in the door-frame leading to the hallway that separated our two rooms, right and left, as Harold's face, red with anger, moved into position between me and the ceiling, blocking out the light from the round florescent fixture that buzzed and buzzed and buzzed throughout our silent dinners, like a thousand dying mosquitoes, one by one flying into an electric zapper at the end of an unbearable summer.

It came, his palm that night, hard and fast and whole, into my chest; only after his face was all I could see, as if that was the important thing: that I knew it was him knocking me off balance, up against the kitchen wall.

Zzt, zzt, zzt, went the light, my mother and I marching like mosquitoes into his path.

I know she was relieved when I finally went to college. Early admission. She had already given up one man for me; was not about to lose another. Not voluntarily, at least.

The month I left, Harold kicked my mother out and kept the house she half paid for. When I visited her that Christmas, she was living in a one-bedroom apartment in Palo Alto, working in a department store selling clothes, again, to her better-off neighbors.

Years later, my mom would pay a lawyer thirty-three percent of the settlement she got from the lawsuit, which in the end was less than she'd originally put into Harold's house. But at least they didn't go to trial, because then she'd have had to pay her lawyer forty percent. The money left over was just enough for her to buy a brand new jeep and ship the entirety of her belongings back to Baobique. I helped her pack, just before starting law school.

The thing that frustrated me most about my mom was that she never learned, she didn't pay attention when life left her clues. I told her when she moved back to Baobique, started fixing up Godwyn, I told her point blank, so she couldn't misunderstand: *Remember what happened with Harold. Don't do anything with Godwyn until it's yours.* But she never listened.

As I pulled into the drive on Mira Vista, the stranger with the gentle telephone voice opened the front door. He waited patiently for me on his porch as I cut the engine, smiled wide and fake, and stepped into the cold morning air toward what was once our home.

From the top of the stairs, the man smiled back, whispered loud, but not loud enough to break into voice. *She's fallen asleep on the couch.*

After I woke my mom and shepherded her into the passenger seat, the man looked deep into my eyes, placed his hand on my shoulder, and confided, *My mother had Alzheimer's, too. It's okay.*

I looked at him. And left. Waited until we were safely in the car. *What, in God's name, was that? That man thought you'd lost your mind, Mom. And right now, I'm inclined to agree.*

She puckered her lips in disgust, sucked her teeth, and looked out the passenger window. *No one is ever on my side. I feel I have no family left,* she said.

We took the alternate highway back to San Francisco. Edgewood Road. San Mateo. Half Moon Bay. Designer houses perched on their very own crests, peering past the highway to the reservoir, and the other way, to the bay. The wind combed the hair of the matted perennials thick, thick along the hillsides, just like in Baobique, the knit of the tree cover buffering our anger.

* * *

As soon as we walked through the door to my studio, she was at it again, picking up the phone, dialing long distance straight to Baobique, straight to Granny.

Mama, it's me . . . I need to know when I can come back home . . .

I couldn't hear my grandmother on the other end of the cables, fiber optic, buried far below her ocean floor, that brought her words to Oakland, the receiver pressed against my mother's ear with a hand beginning to tremble. But my mom started to beg: *We'll do anything you want . . .*

That did it. I grabbed the phone from her limp wrist, demanded an explanation from the other end. *Granny, this is Jean. I need to know what's happening. What is my mom talking about? Why can't she come home?*

The receiver to my ear, I heard her even through the distance. As skilled a politician as Uncle George ever was, Granny ignored my questions and answered instead with her own agenda. *Apparently, the two of you don't care that you have dragged this family's name through the dirt. But I do. And I will not stand by to see you and your mother finish us off.*

Okay, Granny. If you have something to say to me, say it. I'm not sure what we're talking about. I lied, waited to see if she had the courage to really air our laundry.

And she did. Granny, tough as nails. *Oh, you know exactly what I'm talking about. That Hill girl came to George's funeral on purpose. Just to rub your dirty business in our noses. But I tell you, I will not have it. You and your mummy can stay in California. This family does not need the likes of you.*

Death definitely brings out the worst in people. Yet, I must admit, I have never known anyone in my family, ever, to rise in a crisis. All of us sink, deep down, into our most primitive ways of being, ways that normally we see fit to hide.

What do you mean? What does my mom have to do with this? What did she ever do to you? You can't take Godwyn from her.

You take me for a fool, don't you. I give that house to her and it goes straight to you as soon as she's gone. Not a chance. Not a chance, I tell you.

That was why my mom needed the plane ticket. That was why she packed all her belongings, tried first for the safety of Auntie Lil in England. That was why she'd slept outside on a stranger's porch; told me that morning she had no family left. It was all because of me. And Susan.

I slammed down the phone. Turned to my mother, collapsed and coughing, amidst her bags on the futon, bloodred eyes streaming tears.

I couldn't leave her alone. Not like that. But Cynthia's hearing was in two days and I had to prepare. I had to get back to the office.

I've always had this idea in my head I can't seem to shake: that I'm too weak to be an attorney; that if tested, my grit would prove unable to withstand the first strong wind, and I'd crumble or wilt, like my mother after the divorce. I'd run to my bed at the first knock of adversity, like she always did when her men left her. Indeed, those days I did sleep a lot.

But the thing that has always allowed me, ever since law school, to argue a point in public, has been this simple truth: As an advocate, the words coming out of my mouth are, by definition, not for me—they are for someone less able to articulate them.

When I was a kid in elementary school, every year on Dr. Martin Luther King's birthday, we went to the library to be read to about the 1960s, his work, his struggles, his assassination.

I remember thinking, the only little brown head in the library, that I sure was glad Dr. King had won that fight before I was old enough to know a world of segregation, of Jim Crow. I mouthed the words to those songs, feeling weak and tiny, sure that, if tested, I'd prove unable to fight for myself, much less for my whole race. I was always glad, on those days, when our teachers assured us the civil rights movement had already been won and we no longer had to worry about such injustice.

There are two types of wrong in law. There are actions that are wrong because they are inherently bad, and there are actions that are wrong simply because they are somehow inconvenient. It is the difference between killing someone and making a right-hand turn against a red light in the wrong state.

We would move to dismiss at the outset of the hearing on the ground that, in light of new law, Linda was no longer Sadie's adoptive parent and, because of that, her complaint no longer stated a legal wrong. She had no rights regarding Sadie. No recourse in this forum.

But we still needed a backup plan. Just in case. There was always a chance things wouldn't go as anticipated. All it would take to make parentage an issue, ripe for argument, would be for the judge to allow both sides to speak. There'd be a tug of war: between the cases that helped Cynthia, saying that a child belongs only to the one who bore her; and the cases that helped Linda, saying parents are those who act like them.

Granted, Linda's line of cases lacked Cynthia's strength of precedent, but not necessarily its merit. So I needed to organize our facts, make a plan for their admission into evidence, anticipate responses.

I had to get back to the office. My mother was a heap on the floor of my studio and I had no time for indulgence. I had to get to work.

After her stunt sleeping on the stranger's front porch, though, and then the call to Granny, I couldn't leave her alone. She'd have to come with me.

I squatted at her side, explained quietly and firmly, *Mom, I have to go to work . . . You'll have to come with me today.* No touch. *Mom, we have to go now. Get up off the floor.*

When I was a child, I used to listen from the top of the stairs to my mother in bed, on the phone. Wait for her to get up on her own. But she never did. Not until Harold. For all those years I had so much patience.

But not anymore; I screamed, *Get up! Get off the floor!* Then stopped. Stared at us both, caught like my father's fist, raised to strike.

Again, we drove in silence, crossed back over the same bridge the opposite way. Oakland to San Francisco. Gaining no ground.

If I could just get in a good two or three hours, I would be okay. But the fog had thickened into rain and slowed our progress.

By the time we reached my building, the support staff had gone to lunch, the attorneys busy behind closed doors. Good. No need to explain my mother's presence, her bloodshot eyes.

She'd never seen my office, my diplomas professionally framed, didn't comment on them or on anything else as I motioned her to the low leather couch against the far wall, through which she could see a view of Oakland, back across the bay—if she ever looked up.

This is my office. I fished for a crumb of recognition I'd done something noteworthy, sought validation though I knew I shouldn't.

My mom lay down on the couch, prepared for sleep as the rain misted my window, floor to ceiling. Dark clouds comforted me with their closeness. I turned to my cabinet, pulled the file, sat at my desk.

The documents that composed Cynthia and Linda's life together were these: joint title to their flat; statements from their single account at Wells Fargo; Sadie's birth certificate; the court order from Linda's second-parent adoption; Linda's will; her tax returns claiming Sadie as a full dependent; photos of Sadie and their pet corgi.

Two lives as intertwined as any man and wife; all those documents, except one, arguing Linda's case, supporting the fairness of shared custody. Right on top sat my copy of the *Sharon S.* decision, invalidating any legal significance at their attempt to simulate a marriage. That is what it meant to be gay: to secure your whole emotional being with anchors invisible to the rest of the world. The ballast of second-parent adoptions cut loose by the court.

I became an attorney because I wanted to speak for people with voices smaller than mine. I should've been Linda's attorney, not Cynthia's. It was as if the woman Cynthia had been all those years was merely a masquerade.

Ten years ago, I thought I knew what it meant to be a lesbian. I thought it was about sex, about sleeping with women. Gender taboos. But what was the mere touching of tongues compared to all those plans, Linda and Cynthia's, before their break?

I rose from my desk, heavy with the weight of the words I was to speak on behalf of my client, walked toward the kitchenette to boil water for tea. As I passed the reception area, I glanced toward my secretary's desk, upon which sat a tiny gold frame, white embroidery on black cloth that read: *No man is worth crying over. And the one that is, won't make you cry.*

The law states two kinds of wrong. Which one, though, was at hand?

My mother slept on the couch.

Paper can't speak for itself. The organizing of documents not enough, I called Cynthia in to run through her testimony should the court deny our initial Motion to Dismiss. On their own, those pieces of paper—their title in joint tenancy, wills and adoption orders—couldn't be considered by the court until they were admitted into evidence through the words of a living, breathing witness. Someone to verify their significance.

I walked into the reception area to grab a few *Sunset* magazines from the coffee table to keep my mom occupied if she were to wake. She liked the landscaping ideas, often turned to them for inspiration at Godwyn. For years she experimented with rows of purple cabbage—edible landscaping—out back by the shed, but the villagers from Sommerset kept stealing them for soup. Every Christmas I got her a new subscription.

When Cynthia arrived, I put on my professional façade, a wide, wide smile.

Cynthia! Hello. Welcome. I reached for her right hand with both of mine, magazines momentarily set aside on my secretary's desk, right next to her plaque and its meticulous stitching. I picked up the magazines and motioned Cynthia down the hall to my office. *Can I get you anything before we start? Some coffee, water? It will take us some time this morning.*

No. No. I'm okay. Just a little nervous. I didn't realize I'd get this nervous.

She looked smaller than the last time I saw her. Less sure of herself. Her hands were trembling when I took them in mine.

It was my job to put her at ease, to radiate a confidence in the strength of her case and the righteousness of our strategy even if I didn't believe in it, to infuse her with the ability to step up on the stand the next day, sure of foot.

I threw my head back, laughed a deep, dismissive laugh, told her, *Good. That means you're ready to get to work. Let's give that extra energy something productive to do.*

I placed my free arm formally around Cynthia's shoulders—a coach calming her player's pre-game jitters—and entered my office to find my mother snoring from the couch.

At that point, I couldn't afford to let my client see even the thinnest fissure in my composure. I was constantly to assure her I had everything under control, or she'd lose faith in me, in her case, in herself; it was my job to make sure that didn't happen.

I gestured to the snoring lump on my low-lying couch and, with sarcastic formality, introduced my mother: *Cynthia, this is my mother, Sophia Pascal Souza.* I placed the magazines on the table next to the couch, retrieved Cynthia's file from my desk. *Let us now proceed to the conference room.*

My mom snorted in her sleep.

Cynthia smiled, relaxed a bit; perhaps comforted by seeing that tie to the maternal in her lawyer's life on the eve of her fight for exclusive control over her own daughter.

We entered the conference room and started reviewing the documents she'd need to identify, and explain, at the hearing.

I picked up the first piece of paper, the title in joint tenancy to their flat, just off Ocean Beach. Joint tenancy with rights of survivorship, meaning if one of them were to die, the other would inherit that house, as opposed to the relatives of the deceased. After their breakup, Linda moved in with her brother, but still covered half the mortgage through automatic monthly payments directly to the bank, because she still owned half the house and wanted to make sure Sadie's living situation stayed stable.

I handed Cynthia the title. *We're going to explain to the judge that even if she disregards the law as it stands, Sadie is still better off in your sole custody because you were always, as you continue to be, not only her biological mother, but also the central parental figure in her world.*

I continued, *Linda will argue that documents like this,* pointing to the paper in her hand, *this title in joint tenancy, proves that she cared as much about Sadie's stability and future as you did. In fact, didn't Linda pay for most of the down payment?*

Cynthia's eyes widened, and her mother's chest, heavy and low, began to rise and fall faster and faster. She felt attacked, faltered. *It's not my fault that Linda makes more money than I do. She always has. I didn't think this was going to be about money, or houses, or things like that.* She looked over at the stack of documents I'd compiled, looked to be on the verge of tears. Started to shake.

I raised my hand in front of her face to stop her speech, index finger in the air for emphasis. *Perfect. Stop right there. That's exactly how you will respond tomorrow. I jotted down some notes on my legal pad. Okay, now tell me the things that aren't about money that you give to Sadie. And remember, I'm on your side. The attorney tomorrow won't be. So before you answer each question, take a slow, deep breath. Practice being calm with me.* I reached out, placed my hand on her shoulder, offered her the detachment of someone with less at stake than the loss of a child.

Well . . . life. I gave her life. Isn't that enough? Half question. Half not. Her tone anchored by a mother's indignation.

Ha! My mom's laugh, piercing the calm I'd created with Cynthia, shot from behind us, grazed my temple. She had followed us into the conference room. *Ha! You're asking Jean?! She doesn't even know how to be a daughter. How could she tell you what it is to be a mother?*

Cynthia and I were silent, not knowing what to say.

My mom lit into me with all she had: *You act like you're her family. You treat her better than you do your own mother.* She pursed her lips, looked at us in disgust, sucked her teeth. And, on the exhale, fell to the floor.

When I was little, my mother's hands, combing through my hair, seemed so big. But as I ran to her side, grabbed her wrist for a pulse, I saw how small she actually was.

Oh my God! Mom! Mom! Wake up! Get up! I slapped her face two or three times. Probably too hard.

Cynthia was at the phone. *Should I call an ambulance?*

I don't know. I don't know. I began to panic, started to scream, *Mom! Mom!* My lungs were working, moving in and out, at double-speed, but I couldn't breathe.

Three weeks earlier, my mother's younger brother passed in her arms. *George is dead! George is dead!* That's how they said it in Baobique.

There in my office, the storm finally hit California. Cynthia left the phone, ran over to us on the floor, and took my mother from my arms. She laid her flat and blew, simply blew on her face.

My mom came to.

Jean, go get me something citrus from the kitchen. And slice it in half. Cynthia's voice was soft, metered, but firm. I sat and stared at the two of them. Cynthia needed to tell me again. *Jean. Go.*

I went.

By the time I returned to the conference room with the two halves of orange, my mother was sitting upright against the wall. Cynthia, sitting next to her, took a piece of the fruit from my hand and placed it in my mom's. *Hold this under your nose. It will bring you back.*

The inside of the orange was red. Like my mother's eyes, staring straight through me.

I fell back into the closest chair alongside the large oak conference table; felt as though I had the wind knocked out of me.

I pressed the other half of the orange under my own nose, stared at my mom, collapsed for the second time in two days.

My mother was unraveling right before my eyes. How could I not shelter her?

I can't do it. My words surprised me as much as them. They stared up at me. *Cynthia, I have to take my mother home. She's obviously not well . . . But we are not ready yet for tomorrow's hearing. We've barely begun to go through your testimony. We'll have to get a continuance. I'll ask opposing counsel to agree to an additional week. I'll just tell them the truth. I have to deal with a family emergency . . . I'm sorry.*

And I think that for the rest of my life, the sharp smell of citrus will be enough to stop me in my tracks. Sometimes a big red flag means blood.

Chapter 12

THE DAY I WAS SUPPOSED TO BE trying the biggest hearing of my young career, I wasn't even close. The judge had granted our request for a continuance. By then, those things that lived in the ground would have begun to eat through the wood veneer of my uncle's casket out back beneath the guava and spreading baobab trees at Godwyn. Translucent lizards the size of my fist sat atop his gravestone, listened to the low growl of the waves crashing along the reef, watched the thunder clouds rolling in with their storms, the rough Atlantic turning green with the coming of hurricanes.

My mother's imbalance and Granny's iron fist tipped us to the ground. The two of us tumbled to the airport, onto a plane, and headed toward Baobique.

I did not want to go. More than anything in the world, I did not want to go and face her family. Last they'd seen me—rolling around behind Godwyn with Susan—they'd asked me, in no uncertain terms, to take my American morals and leave their island. But my mom's voice, hoarse from her sore throat, had no force against Granny's anymore. And she couldn't afford to lose another home.

We were entering the last leg of our trip, just hours away, at the international airport in San Juan.

My mother was fast asleep across two of the black plastic and metal chairs near our departure gate.

I left my post at the top of that particular staircase, hoped no one would try to steal her passport—or at least would catch her oozing pink eye if they did.

In San Juan, I took all I could get: wandered the corridors eliciting simple nods of recognition with my mismatched eyes and loopy curls. There, I looked like I belonged. Keeping silent when addressed—by a lost traveler, a janitor, a banker—they greeted me in Spanish, continued until the blankness in my expression gave me away. It was only then they treated me as an American, switched to English.

After using up nearly one of my two hours in the airport, I took a seat opposite my mother, among the other Baobiquens bound for Beckford Hall.

The first time I flew to Baobique with my mom, I was ten. She'd managed to stay awake the entire trip. She'd also managed to remember I needed a passport and sat me under the big electric dryer, pink plastic curlers rolled into four lines from my forehead to my neck, for two hours the night before I had to take my photo, styling my hair in two cascading ringlets on either side of my head, so Granny wouldn't complain when she asked to see my passport. That was the same year she sent me to school on Picture Day at Lincoln with my hair completely uncombed, deciding not to purchase the results either because the ten dollars was better spent on cereal, eggs, and low-fat milk, or because she couldn't possibly claim a child who could look so unkempt. Small wonder she cut all my hair off before we actually left for Baobique; my mom was not up to the task of remaining my hairdresser.

When we arrived at Beckford Hall that trip, the customs officer didn't recognize my mom's face or my father's last name, still on her passport, and sent us to the foreigner's line because I was from the wrong place: the United States.

Maybe that was why she only spoke *of* me that trip, instead of ever *to* me, and laughed along with Uncle Martin's wife when their maid tried to dress me in the morning and I ran down the hall screaming because some strange woman was trying to remove my nightclothes.

I woke in Granny's second bedroom at Tours, marred head to toe with mosquito welts from the hole at the top of her old netting, to the sound of Uncle George's booming voice, looking just for me, chanting: *Where . . . is . . . Jean? . . . Where . . . is . . . Jean?*

I ran out to Granny's living room in my lavender, no-sleeved pajamas and short, short hair to the wrong uncle. He wasn't Uncle Charles from Canada. He wasn't anyone I knew at all. But he smiled so wide when he saw me, I forgave him on the spot.

It was nice to be noticed. My parents had just divorced, and by that time my dad had already started forgetting to pick me up on the weekends.

It was that first meeting, way back then, that I claimed Uncle George as my own. A replacement for my own absentee father.

I would have followed Uncle George to the ends of the earth, like a duckling imprinting on the first thing it saw. It was as if Uncle George, and all those mosquitoes, were the only ones happy I'd come at all.

The Beckford Hall airport is at the northern end of Baobique, close to Granny. Most people prefer to fly into Beckford Hall because it is much safer than the De Canne airport, near Bato, the capital and busiest town at the southernmost tip of the island, where the wind off the sea can flip a plane.

In San Juan there are no worries like that. The airport in Puerto Rico is big, more like the ones in the U.S. than on the little islands. And so there I transitioned slowly to my mother's Third World, not yet required to let go of all my luxuries.

I studied each face in the Baobique section of the airport. From there on out, I would be watched. Every one of those people, save one or two white American or European scuba divers, were Baobiquen, and had already begun watching me, across from my lump of slumbering mother, wondering how I came to be a Pascal.

You are a Pascal, a middle-aged man with a receding hairline and tiny graying curls, cropped close against dark, dark skin, addressed me with an accent belying long stints in North America. He pointed to my mom, took the seat directly adjacent to mine. *If she is your mother, you must be a Pascal.*

I didn't want to play nice with someone who obviously knew my mother's family, someone who'd probably side with them if he found out the truth about me. But he knew my name; I had no excuse for reticence. I conceded, *I am.*

I am Louis Petion. He settled in for extended conversation, left me no out. *I am sorry to hear about George. I attended his burial last week. They did a beautiful job of it, out at Godwyn.*

That's my mother's house. I pointed across the aisle. *George was my uncle.*

He smiled, small. Encouraged. *You know, I was in politics with your uncle. I was on the other side, Peoples'. He was Liberty.*

Admittedly, I was curious . . . *Did you know Prime Minister Hill?*

Oh yes. I worked directly with him for some time.

I've never met any Socialists on Baobique. I only know my mother's family.

Mr. Petion scooted closer in his black plastic airport chair, looked around him conspiratorially, lowered his voice to almost a whisper. *You know . . . some people think his heart attack was no accident. There were rumors of an assassination. Hill was a very rad-*

ical man. Too radical for many. He wanted the public cemetery, you know. His family went against his wishes when they buried him on their private estate.

My uncle told me Hill was once imprisoned in Canada for instigating Black Power demonstrations.

That is true. I was there. It was during university. But what is wrong with speaking your mind? Even if it means they'll lock you up or kick you out, like they did to Hill?

They kicked him out of university?

He laughed, tossed his head back, his chin to the sky. *Young Pascal, they kicked Hill out of Canada. He was a troublemaker, I'll give him that. He made people very uncomfortable.*

Mmmm. I can understand that.

Mr. Petion smiled big then, as if I were joking, winked my way. *But Pascal, what could a sweet young woman like yourself know of trouble-making, na?*

I changed the subject fast, fast, rose to wake my mother for boarding. *Well, I would have liked to meet Prime Minister Hill. I'm sorry I never got the chance.*

When there are too many twenty-five-seaters flying in and out of Beckford Hall, its single runway used by both the arriving and departing planes, sometimes you have to circle the island to bide time.

Normally the planes fly through the valley and land toward the sea, rather than toward the mountains. Since it was overcast in the valley, we landed toward the mountains. But the winds are bad that way, the runway short, and there's a chance you might crash into the rock.

We didn't. So everyone on the plane burst out clapping the moment we touched down. Outside the oval windows of our plane, I could see a storm coming, dark and gray. In the foreground, each leaf of the long coconut fronds moving separately in the wind, reflecting leftover light.

We hadn't called Granny to tell her we were coming to address her threats about adding my uncles as heirs to Godwyn. No one in the family knew we were there. So no one was waiting to pick us up. I'd booked the tickets the night before, after I'd gotten the call that the judge had granted us the continuance in Cynthia's case.

Mr. Petion would not hear of letting us take a taxi.

His brother, come to pick him up, threw my backpack and all my mom's bags on the flatbed of his truck, ushered us into his cab, but did not speak. The brother climbed onto the flatbed with the bags. Mr. Petion took the wheel.

My mother, between us, was utterly useless, moving only when told to, from one seat to the next, saying nothing. I was embarrassed; me, not even Baobiquen, calling on help like that from a stranger.

Along the way, a tinge of rust on all things metal: red and green tin roofs, cars, street signs, fences, empty aluminum cans strewn by the roadside. Red Stripe. And Fanta.

We drove mostly in silence, half awkward, half not; pulled up the drive at Godwyn, the crotons and small palms leading us to the car port.

Outside the truck, Mr. Petion's brother handed me my backpack. I asked him, *Can I help with the gas?* Reached for my wallet.

They laughed at my *foolishness.* And asked me how long I'd be visiting.

Until I can talk some sense into my grandmother, I joked.

Ha ha! Into Granny Pascal? Then you'll never leave! Mr. Petion joked back.

He pressed his business card into my palm. An accountant in Bato. *Call me if you need anything, young Pascal. I will be back soon.*

They had another hour on the windy road south.

Chapter 13

ALMOST A YEAR HAD PASSED since I'd set foot on
Godwyn. It was the last place Susan and I'd made love,
before we got caught and Uncle George requested my
departure, half-paralyzed, from Granny's second bedroom.
Patriarchs buried in its breast, the house my mother wanted to
keep as home. Her crumbling, wooden Godwyn: plastic on rotting
cedar planks to keep the outside out; plastic on antique chairs,
over the armoire, to keep them dry just one more rainy season;
bats in the attic; rats in the crawl space below, where the dogs
slept. Yet, all with an elegance calling out from its front porch, its
red tin roof and deep purple bougainvillea, all demanding their
due respect. It might merely be a matter of time before the next
strong winds of the season take down a weight-bearing wall, but
there is something more to that house than its structure. Godwyn
stands, time itself.

The wind from the coming storm wrapped me with its long
arms; hugged me tight, tight; squeezed the breath from my lungs.
Baobique had me once again, and I feared it would never let go.

But my mom seemed to have lost at least a touch of her iner-
tia. She wandered off, out past the graves, as if ordered by some
silent voice that it was time to switch seats.

I let her go: down the dirt path, reddish-brown between

green, stopping only for the sharpest of thorns or sticks beneath her feet, padding her way to the edge of memory; a girl, once again, taking along a dog and a cutlass, even though the path was overused by the squatters in Grampy's garden; through the small guava trees, bananas, and tall arching coconuts, she'd make her way in the rain-wet bush to where she could see. When she got there, she'd stand silent, holding the dog tight, tight, so he wouldn't break her peace. And she'd look out over the tall grass and thin trees, across the valley to the next mountain, and the next, and the next. And she'd lean on her Morne Volcan. Rest.

Behind her, the constant roll of the Atlantic, its soft call never leaving her ears.

She passed from my sight.

I turned to Godwyn, unlocked first the top, then the bottom of my mother's locks. The entrance more shutter than door, I twisted the long wooden arm that acted as a knob, pointed it straight up, and pushed through to the dining room. Yesterday's doors. Bright green against a whitewash of walls.

Like the door, the shutters throughout the house had been closed tight from people, animals, and wind, but it was getting dark, and no sign yet of the dogs, so I only opened the window with glass, the one in my mom's room. From her bed I saw the sun setting over the rough Atlantic, out past the guava trees, the baobabs, and the graves. I had never known Godwyn to hold more than one body. But it wasn't just Grampy anymore. Uncle George was out there, too.

In my head, I could almost hear my grandmother weeks before, how she would have been the day they buried her son, such an important son, next to the body of her husband in this little place.

I could almost hear the wind. The ocean. And it was as if I were there, squatting at the side of the house, digging my fingers into the ground to pull up ginger my mom would boil and sweeten for beer.

I heard Granny, still in my thoughts, from the house: *These girls are so stupid. They can't do anything right. I told them to put the paper serviettes out on the table, and look, they've put out the cloth napkins! Here, take these back to the kitchen and bring me the stack of paper serviettes. People will be coming soon. Look at the table! Oh my God, that dog is in the house . . . People will be coming!*

I pulled a slow, full breath to the bottom of my lungs, held it until it was no longer needed, let it seep out on its own. Wrestled for control. With the next inhalation, not as deep and more metered, my thoughts plunged my head, wet, toward the bottom of the ocean, and the rest of me followed. The slick of the water against my arms and legs and pushing hands oiled my descent into the coral at Tours Beach, masking depths I could not fathom. Coming to the surface, the ripples of the water licked my face with their tiny tongues.

I could hear Susan, too, the night before Uncle Martin— small banana—and Mr. Williams followed us out through the bush, waited, watched until they'd had their fill. I could almost hear her whisper softly in my ear, *We don't have much time. Please. No one is watching.* We'd been right there. On my mother's bed. I kept thinking I'd seen someone outside the shutters, kept thinking I'd heard something just outside the door as she lay on top of me, removed her clothes and mine under the white cotton sheet I kept pulling back up every time her movements pushed it off. Her long fingers grabbing at the back of my arched neck, claiming me hers with each quick breath. Her mouth on mine; her hands gripping, pushing, pulling. Our bodies pressed so tight together I could feel the blood in her veins. Yet my eyes never leaving that window. Distracted.

* * *

Lightning pulsed outside the bedroom window and I was not myself—eyes wide and open; subsided, and I was back—closed. I sat at the edge of the bed, lay back.

In the streets of Bato above my uncle's law practice, my youngest cousins yelled out from their second-floor balcony to men who lived on the streets—*Buller! Buller!*—ducked back inside before they were seen. *Bullers* are poor male prostitutes; my cousins, respectable children among the island's elite.

My mind drifted toward fatigue. I remembered the man with the bad eye from Sommerset I'd seen during my last visit, saw him slip through the open window, felt his hands closing in around my neck, closing in between my legs. He slipped through while my guard was down, tore off my costume—my heterosexual façade— left me bare and exposed in front of my whole family, all of whom just stood there laughing, letting him grab me, place his one good eye and two strong hands on my sleeping skin.

Chapter 14

THE DOGS BARKED ME AWAKE from under the open window. Outside it was pitch black, except for a sliver of moon on the water far below, fast clouds moving past.

My heart hit my throat, stole my breath on its way up: They could not have arrived on their own.

Barking, barking.

Out there, in the country, I voiced a cautious yell . . . *Mom!* Received no reply.

Rascal and Lucia had quieted down but I still heard their movements in the front, by the carport. If they were alone, they would have been here already, running muddy inside the house.

I reached under the pillow, felt for the harmless handgun with shaky fingers, found it, and took hold.

Who's there?

A voice from the bottom of the drive. *Hello, hello! Young Pascal, it is Mr. Petion. I've found your mummy's dogs . . . And I've a friend for you to meet.*

Embarrassed, I slipped the pistol back underneath the pillow, padded over to the still-open front door and halfway down the drive to meet them in my bare feet, the dogs at my heels, turning red with mud.

It's a good thing those dogs remember your smell. A tall, lanky stranger in slacks and a button-down dress shirt like the one Uncle Martin wore to the beach the last time I was here extended his free hand to mine and we shook. His mannerisms vaguely familiar—something about his easy smile.

I'm Jean. Souza. Sophie Pascal's daughter from California. My name meant nothing without that point of reference. *Have we met before? I feel I know you from somewhere.*

Mr. Petion shared his friend's easy smile, let me in on their secret. *This is Leonard Hill, my business partner. I am godfather to his second child, Susan.*

Hill looked me straight in the eyes. Seeing me prone, perhaps, on top his daughter, in the dirt, doing our filthy nonsense. Maybe he was there to get back at me for touching Susan.

My knees grew weak, unstable. *If I were a true Pascal*, I stammered, *I'd have something to offer you . . . some coconut juice, a snack of fried plantain.* I clenched and unclenched my hands behind me, backpedaled toward the house, tried to stay calm, feet on the ground in the cleared bush, and continued, *I'm sorry I have nothing for you.*

I didn't think I had time to reach the gun. Rascal and Lucia, still at my side, knew the men too well to attack. I had worked myself into some mess. Who was I to go there, armed with only my mother's last name, two strikes against me—what I'd done and who knew it. My eyes began to tear.

I was treading water. Barely. Something in their look made me suspect they could see my arms flailing underneath the surface.

You came back, na. For your mummy's house. To me, that has Pascal written all over it . . . George's funeral was the first Susan's been back to Baobique in a year, and your grandmother made such a fuss! It was Mr. Hill who spoke.

Maybe they weren't the other side. I broke. *Look. I'm sorry. But I don't see my mother and I have to find her. She hasn't been well of late . . .*

94 • a simple distance

My mother was missing again and I couldn't negotiate Godwyn without her. Even if I'd known how to unlock her phone, I couldn't call the police. That's not how you solve your problems there.

Apparently enlisting their help, I asked them: *Where did you find my mother's dogs?* They hadn't been here when Mr. Petion dropped us off from the airport.

We didn't find them at all. They found us. Met us at the edge of the road and your mummy's drive. Down by the access road.

The access road had been cut by Grampy when he got the idea about the bay trees. They grow exceptionally well in Baobique.

The only thing I remember about bay, growing up, was not to eat the leaves in the spaghetti sauce. But in Baobique it makes rum. Grampy had twenty of their forty acres at Godwyn covered with bay. Bay got him the land at Milieu, got Uncle George and Uncle Martin educated in England; Uncle Charles, in North America.

The access road cuts all the way through the estate, runs clear to the port at Sommerset. And the rough types there.

I need to find her. I went to my backpack, fished for my running shoes, sunk deep to the bottom, rooted them out, forced my feet in, laced fast. *I need a flashlight, or something.*

You cannot walk that road at this time of night, you are not accustomed to its footing. Mr. Hill tried to tell me what to do. He must have thought I was Susan. Continued, *And a storm is coming soon.*

I noticed, then, the banging shutters of my mother's open window—began to panic. Storms could get big that time of year.

I was brusque because I was scared, and they needed to know I was serious. I grabbed the flashlight and my mother's machete off the hook by the back door, where she always kept it, cut them down to size, told them: *You are not my father. And I have to find my mom. She's all I have.*

With that I was out the door, off and running through a tangle of thin branches and thick red mud, cutting my way through the overgrown bush that would obscure the access road even were it light out; Rascal and Lucia at my feet, chasing the scent of my sweat.

It began to rain but I couldn't stop. I had no choice. This road was in my blood and I followed it downhill. No staying dry anymore. Not for me. If my mother was lost, then so was I. In the middle of my family's forest, it stormed all around me—swinging away with a cutlass to clear a path just big enough to let me through.

When Uncle George was my age, he had just returned to Baobique with his law degree and two eyes toward politics. During that year's hurricane season, he got stranded once in Tete Queue, took shelter in the nearest shack with the little old woman who bakes the bread there. But the winds were fierce and began lifting the tin panels. So Uncle George climbed up to the ceiling and held the roof together with his bare hands.

The old woman had no teeth, but her jaws won Uncle George his first magistrate position; so much thanking she did when he came around every morning to buy Granny's bread—such a mama's boy.

After that Granny always got free loaves of bread. And Uncle George had Tete Queue in his palm.

Valerie would slice the bread with sharpened knives kept counted and locked in Granny's pantry drawer with all the other amenities of her class.

I made my slow way, frantic, with my mother's machete down Grampy's access road. If I'd stopped chasing her, pressed the blade in my right hand hard against my skin to let leak her blood from me, my heart, beating fast, fast, would've had nothing left to push against.

Odd how, with her lost in the dark like that, my wants and fears turned out to be the same thing: her hand rough through my curls. Without her weight, I'd have been adrift in a storm. No ballast to keep me upright.

Turn off da light, na. A whisper, low and unfamiliar, interrupted my lack of progress, mired in the middle of the old road.

Out there, alone. So close to Sommerset. What was I thinking? The flashlight had given me away. My heart was in my throat.

Da light. Again.

No! Who are you? There was no way I was turning it off. In the dark I was defenseless. I scanned the trees with the white from the light beam, reflecting rainy static. My searching stopped cold on the man with the sewn eyelid, not two feet to my left. Before I could say anything else, he knocked the flashlight and the cutlass to the ground, locked a strong wet palm tight on my mouth.

I couldn't believe what was happening. His hand on my mouth; I couldn't scream. His arm at my midsection; I couldn't hit. But I kicked; hard with adrenaline. Broke free. And ran.

I heard him shouting from behind: *Watch out! Watch out!*

He may have been stronger, but I was faster. By far. And I was gone, running with two hands free to push away branches, and just the night. Eyes undistracted by the flashlight's narrow beam— its false security; I moved fast.

On my own again, me and my beating heart. Those dogs nowhere in sight. Utterly useless.

My mind would have liked to wander, wonder how on earth I ended up there, soaked through in the middle of the forest, when just days before I was sitting safe in the coffee shop at the corner, nursing a latte—the only real danger, a hurt feeling or two.

I would have liked to reflect on how these two worlds came to collide in me, violent like the crashing of continents. Find the words for just the proper spin to recount this story at the office, where everyone else who traveled to the Caribbean went for vacation. This was no vacation; it was the hardest work I'd done in years—going back there, simply showing my face.

But they wouldn't understand that at the office, and up ahead I thought I saw a light. It brought me back to the night, the trees around me, the rain drumming its steady rhythm on countless fronds.

My eyes had accustomed themselves to the dark; without the flashlight, I was at an advantage. Quietly as possible, I moved forward.

I heard voices. Men.

The lights were three: two together, one roving.

An engine started up.

The roving beam scanned.

As I moved closer: a voice I knew. *Hello, hello . . . young Pascal!*

It was Mr. Petion.

Jean! And Mr. Hill.

Thank God! I was not going to die in the jungle, get attacked by Granny's "dreds," or fall off a cliff. That cliff only as steep as I chose, I cut it down to child's play, called out, *I'm here! I'm here!* as the flashlight and I made our way toward each other.

Mr. Hill's voice soothed me in the dark, eased back my breath. *You were headed the wrong way, Pascal, this road leads you nowhere you'd want to go, just to a blind cove and its drug runners.*

I argued back, defensive, yet groping my wet perimeter for his outstretched hand. *But this road leads straight to Sommerset. My grandfather cleared it for better access to the port, to export his bay leaves. Uncle George took off six months of his law practice to help.*

They laughed. Petion answered, *I am sorry to inform you, Jean, but an extension has been added since your grampy's time . . .*

This branch leads only to some speedboats I don't think would welcome you, busy with cargo worth much more than bay these days.

I was expecting the soft hand of Mr. Hill, but as the flashlight and I met, it was a rough one that grabbed my arm.

A 'oman must take care on dis road at night. It was that man with his eye, again. I screamed loud and shrill, like a goat under attack.

But by that time he knew me, held me still.

It was Hill, his voice, who brought me back to my senses. *So you are a Pascal after all. You, too, judge quick, without knowing. Trust first your clouded eyes.*

His tone had changed to harsh reproach. He continued, flat and dry, out there in the rain, introduced me to the man whose face had haunted my dreams. *Jean Pascal, this is Mr. Bruce. Mr. Bruce, this is Jean Pascal. Perhaps once she stops screaming, she will thank you for looking after her mummy's dogs for her while she was away.*

Mr. Bruce let go my arm. The four of us stood in silence, save the running engine, the drumming rain.

There was nothing I could say to take back the insults I had twice placed at Mr. Bruce's bare feet; me in my eighty-dollar running shoes, soaked through with shame and caked with red clay. But I offered, as quietly as audible, *I am so sorry.*

Thank God it was too dark for them to look me in the eye.

Mr. Petion broke the ice: *Let's go get Ma Pascal.*

As Mr. Bruce and I approached the car, I realized it was my mom's jeep.

I found my voice. *This is my mother's car.*

Hill answered without even a hint of apology, *We heard she wasn't using it this evening.*

I knew enough not to respond right then. I was not so much in their favor as I'd been even an hour before; before I showed my true colors—the Pascal slipping out from under my costume.

But Hill, not quite finished with my punishment, continued as we filed into my mom's jeep and headed toward Sommerset: *Do you know how your uncle's party came to power?*

It was a coup, a bloodless coup. I remembered reading a clipping in Uncle George's living room just after I graduated from college, when I stayed with him in De Canne.

Nearly bloodless, he corrected my history. *There were two deaths. One man was shot. And a baby died from tear gas.*

Mmm. I remember that now. I'd forgotten those two.

The car was silent again, the rain lessening against its roof, high beams clawing at the dark along the bumpy incline of the access road, back toward the pavement of the government-sponsored street heading to Sommerset.

Once on the pavement, Mr. Hill shifted up, told me, as all eyes but mine knew to avert, *That was Mr. Bruce's child. His little girl.*

We drove through the intersection at Sommerset that rested at the mouth of its well-trafficked cove; left through the thinning road, no longer paved, but lined with homes of wood and tin.

The wind had sway with the trees' tall fronds, and there sat my mother on Mr. Williams's porch, with her arms around a rain-soaked goat.

Chapter 15

ONE-MILE IS A STRIP OF ROAD that leads in, toward the mountains, from the sea at Port Commons. It is exactly one mile from start to finish.

Part of me felt as though Granny had always been on her front porch, staring out past the cliff, the muffled crash of the waves below. But I knew she hadn't. I knew she used to make them all walk One-Mile every day for exercise, just before dinner, even when it was too windy and for every step forward it pushed them back two. The exercise was to make them strong. But my mom had trouble keeping up.

They'd walk until the "Y" at the roundabout that goes to either Milieu or deeper, into the forest where the dreds live, grow their cannabis, steal young girls—Granny said.

My mom told me that once when she couldn't keep up, she just sat down right there, low in a ditch along the side of the road—the worst place to be when a storm is coming. And a big one was coming that night.

The rest of them kept going. But Uncle Martin went back for her with a rope. He tied one end around his own waist, the other around my mom's. Dragged her home that way against strong winds.

Granny had Grampy give them both the switch for falling behind. Granny always said the country was no place to be weak.

Uncle Martin said he'd walked that stretch of road more than any other in his entire life, remembered it *like the back of Grampy's hand*: the overgrown soccer field; the bus stop's blue and white cement blocks; Granny Lavall's wooden shack; the forest, close, close; and that rope, burns on their stomachs.

My mom didn't joke about it like Uncle Martin.

Could it have been as simple as giving shelter to a goat in a storm—my mother's apology, as we came to fetch her home? But who was she protecting in her stupor?

We pulled up next to Mr. Williams's house, stopping there in the narrow road, clogged the muddy artery. Mostly walkers, rarely cars, passed through. The rain, by then barely falling, allowed for open doors; through his, one of Mr. Williams's boys, on a stoop in the center of their one room, beneath a dangling cord and its electric bulb.

Mr. Williams leaned against one side of the doorway, greeted the men—Messrs. Hill, Petion, and Bruce—with a nod, ignored me completely.

I returned the favor, left my mother's car for her side, next to the goat. But she didn't seem to see me. And while I wanted her to reach out to me, it was hard enough to extend my own hand, grab hold, help carry her weight.

I had to tug to break her grip on the damn goat, pull her to the backseat of her jeep, lock the door, leave her there.

The men had moved inside and Mr. Hill had the keys to the car. So I had to follow them in, past the porch and its wind-weary stock. As I strode, head high with the false confidence of my family's airs, out the corner of my eye I caught sight of its left hind leg—marred thick with scar.

I blinked it aside, but not really. So the goat had lived, after all. And Mr. Williams had gotten a windfall: Granny's cash and

the goat to boot. The goat was quiet though. That night I was the
only one screaming out, in the bush, for aid.

I crossed the threshold, into Mr. Williams's wooden room,
and all their eyes jerked up at me. The four of them: Hill, Petion,
Williams, and Bruce; huddled together around the single table,
mostly used for dominoes, suddenly looking like it was them
rolling on the ground together out back at Godwyn instead of
Susan and me—doing something equally unspeakable. Caught in
a private act. Embarrassed.

Mr. Hill was first to clear his throat, fish around in his mouth
for something to say, find his tongue.

It's settled, then. He rose from his seat, the others following his
lead. *Come, Jean, let's get your mummy home. She needs to sleep.*

What's going on? I asked, as they filed past me, out the door
and back into the night. But no one answered.

We drove back up the hill, from Sommerset to Godwyn, Mr.
Williams following us in an old Toyota.

At Godwyn, I put my mother to bed. She, falling asleep
before her head hit the pillow that buffered her loaded little gun.
I pulled off her sandals, foot by muddy foot, removed her wet
clothes, covered her up with a white cotton sheet, and left her to
commune with Grampy and Uncle George.

I closed the door behind myself on the way out.

Mr. Williams and Mr. Bruce must have gone back down to
Sommerset. But Hill and Petion had followed me into the house
and made themselves at home while I was with my mom. They'd
pulled out chairs, Orange Fanta, rum, and a cold cooked chicken
from a brown paper bag in the back of Mr. Petion's brother's truck.
They made themselves more comfortable, there in my mother's
dining room, than I would likely be that entire visit.

Mr. Hill told me to get some plates, pepper sauce, and glasses,
rolled his eyes at his friend in mock paternal horror. *She is just like*

Susan, na? These children would have us all eating out of paper bags if it wasn't for us reminding them how to be civilized.

In the kitchen for the place settings, I found the plates next to the window above the counter. Its shutters open for air, I looked out into the night. As our picture window framed my view of the world when I was a child, that one framed my mother's. You could see the mountains: layered and canopied with wide green fronds. You could see the graves, the plum tree, and all the paths that led us everywhere we'd been: chasing Mr. Williams's goat, my mom, Grampy's bay leaves, his ghost.

The first time I met Fatima, grating soursop to pulp for juice, she saw me in my running shorts out that window. She said to me, *Boy, you sure Sophie's girl all right. You've your mummy's legs.*

Back when my mom was young, her legs may not have run like mine, but they carried her swift into trouble. When my uncles would sneak out Grampy's motorcar, push it to the road so they wouldn't be heard, drive themselves, Auntie Clara, and my mom into Bato to make mischief for the night—a two-hour trip back then, top speed—her legs caught the attention of the young school master from the Grenadines.

So even when she'd be so tired she'd nod off the next day during lessons, she never got switched for it. Instead, the school master would slip his hand under the skirt of her school uniform to wake her with his touch.

Before she knew it, he was doing favors for my uncles, lending them turns on his motorbike so they'd say favorable things to Grampy about him. My mom was just seventeen when they married. He was twenty-three. He'd sold his motorbike to buy her engagement ring. But Grampy paid for the rest.

After my parents had moved to the States, Grampy'd ask them, when they'd call, *Why live like a pauper in a strange country when you can live like a king in your own?*

Living like a king in Baobique, though, came attached to strings I guess my father'd rather cut, because they didn't stay there long. Even with that view: forest so green it breathed right along with you; cliffs; the ocean; the single black paved road negotiated by Uncle George, peeking out just around the bend down there.

During rainy season, when the wind picked up, it combed through the fronds, and the trees just swayed, swayed in its wake.

And there I stood, on that precipice, wondering what was next.

Sometimes there is a simple distance through which we must pass before we can even begin. Sometimes that distance is all wound up—tight on itself like a tangle—inside us.

I gathered the plates and glasses, returned to lessening strangers in the dining room.

At the end of our meal as well as the end of the rum, the two men joked about my uncle. *At first*, Hill said, *George didn't look like politics at all*, because he couldn't curse the other politicians in patois. Grampy only ever allowed the King's English to pass from the lips of his children.

They told me they'd take me, in the morning, to Tours. They'd talk to Granny with me. Uncle Martin had already been called, CarCom to CarCom; his morning appearances in Bato continued to the afternoon. They'd stay with us at Godwyn tonight, on the couch and the extra bed.

Whether I liked it or not, they were all I had. So I practiced being calm with them.

Before we turned in, Mr. Petion took me, again, into his confidence, like at the airport earlier that day. Tipsy from rum, he told me they'd received some convincing evidence from Mr. Williams that evening. Mr. Hill was good and ready for a fight with the Pascals because Granny had embarrassed Susan at Uncle George's funeral—wouldn't let her place flowers or pay her respects. He told me Mr. Hill did not like his only daughter to feel she had no place on this island over *some such silly women's business.* The hospital at Port Commons needed a new Chief of Staff and Susan had recently expressed a strong interest in staying on the island, since her residency in Nassau had reached its end. There was also a young engineer in Bato, just back from London, an eligible bachelor Mr. Petion had had his eyes on for his only godchild.

So she was there. Susan was in Baobique.

From the bathroom sink, Mr. Hill called out. He told me not to worry, *the Pascals aren't the only family in Baobique, you know.* Directly to my uncle, Hill shouted out open shutters, *George, your young Pascal is fighting back, man. Fighting back!* His loose chest bouncing from the chuckle. Softer, he added, *And she's not alone, boy. She's not alone.*

There, at the sink, Mr. Hill could have been my Uncle George, readying himself for tomorrow's trial, rinsing his briefs before he went to bed. But Uncle George was lying out back next to Grampy under the guava trees, protected by a layer of red clay from the swift midnight breeze.

Chapter 16

MORNING WOKE ONLY MOMENTS before I did, woke me with wind and the sting of fear in my chest, knocked over a tin wheelbarrow next to the shed. Seemed to me a storm was again approaching. Hurricane season. My stomach was in knots.

Mr. Petion and Mr. Hill wanted some aspirin for their heads. *Perhaps a little too much of the Bajan rum last night,* I suggested, as they washed up. I put the water on to boil for instant coffee.

We took the aging sedan Mr. Williams had driven up behind us from Sommerset the night before, something vaguely familiar in its worn velvet seats, and left my mom, still sleeping, in Fatima's strong hands.

The night before on Mr. Williams's porch, reaching back for her, tugging her body, limp with resignation, to the car, and buckling her in, I'd felt her weight was slowing me down. Never mind I wasn't going anywhere myself—had been stationary for some time.

Mr. Hill drove quick and twisty along the winding coastal road to Tours, hugging corners by instinct—the drop to the left, unthinkable, off those cliffs.

From the backseat, I could see early risers waiting along the side of the road for a lift into Bato, or for the bus—a minivan with an extra row of seats. We drove against the flow of traffic, mostly a handful of trucks. Flatbeds holding more bodies than cargo. It was not banana day, and anyway, banana day was not what it used to be. Not since the European Union took away the British subsidies.

Less curious than anxious, little to lose at this point, I asked Mr. Hill, *How did you know what my grandmother was up to with my mom's house?*

He answered, *This island is smaller than you think, Jean. Valerie, your granny's maid, works for me on the weekends.*

Granny dangled the family house over my mom's head like a carrot, keeping her under foot so there was always someone around to step on. One day she said Godwyn would go to my mom, the next day took it back. All, she said, because of either me and Susan, or a goat, depending on whom she was talking to.

Here's the irony. Not so long before my grandfather acquired his land in Baobique, at Tours, at Godwyn, at Milieu, I would have had a stronger claim to it than either of my grandparents.

Grampy got most of his estates for next to nothing, bought from the last of the British left on the island, long after slavery was outlawed, and living in the West Indies had started to mean that those who'd stayed had gone wild like the Baobiquens themselves.

But Baobique held on to some of the more primitive customs introduced by the Europeans, wrote them into the island's laws. Back then, the ways in which land passed from person to person were governed by a set of statutes under which gradations in the pigment of a person's skin either granted them the right to own property, or took it away, according to a strict hierarchy: white, brown, black.

Years before my mother was born, before my grandfather returned to Baobique with his medical degree from Quebec, one of the coldest Canadian provinces there is, he lived for a long time as the single black man in his town. His landlady only allowed him to see his patients at night, his patients respectable Canadians with unmentionable diseases—communicable only in private. During the day he stayed inside. Slept. But he returned to Baobique with enough money for Tours, Godwyn, and Milieu; he married my grandmother, the daughter of a wash girl from Tete Queue; for three decades he was the island's only physician; and eventually, he drank himself to death. This much I know about Grampy Pascal.

My other grandfather was Portuguese, gave to my father his fair, fair skin and to both of us our green eyes.

Not so long ago, by virtue of nothing more than the color of my dad, I could have simply stepped in, called upon that Chief Justice who'd recently extolled the virtues of my late Uncle George to my grandmother at the courthouse in Bato, and had him sign over Godwyn to me.

But Baobique was crumbling its old ways into the sea, taking with it my mother's family, making us fight over land in which I am undeniably implicated.

We came upon the road of red clay that led down to Tours Beach. Mr. Hill at the wheel of the Toyota, the trees did not part for us. And we passed it by. There for a purpose that day, not a sea bath. Up ahead, Granny's.

He slowed the car, threw me a quick look from the driver's seat, and told me this: *Young Pascal, listen close. Words can be sharp as a cutlass. It doesn't matter if they are true or if they are false, just that they cut. We are going to slice your Granny and Uncle Martin down to their true size. You will have to trust me and remember why you and your mummy flew through all that wind yesterday in that silly little plane with Mr. Petion.*

I had to trust him. I had no one else. It wasn't as if I'd developed a large network of allies and it was up to me to finesse some sort of resolution between my mom and her family. With Uncle George's passing, Granny's general may have been gone but his armies were still amassed. And they did not like my kind.

Mr. Petion: *Facts shift fast as storm clouds in Baobique. You watch, Jean.*

Just after the coup that brought my uncle's party into power, an agreement was signed in the House of Assembly appointing Barrister George Pascal to the office of Chief Minister. Liberty's leader thereafter, Dame Devon, became the first female Prime Minister in the Caribbean. To people in the street, she became *dat steel 'oman*. I do not believe she ever married.

Susan's uncle, Archibald Hill, succeeded Dame Devon as Prime Minister. His party, Peoples, winning out over her more conservative contingent in public elections. Prime Minister Hill's heart attack, the one that coincided with Uncle George's mass effect and occasioned my meeting Susan in Granny's kitchen over ham sandwiches, came just a year into his term of office. His second-in-line was less radical and better liked by the island's old-school Parliament.

The late Prime Minister's brother pulled us up to Granny's front porch, where she sat on her lawn chair waiting. The mood in the car had shifted, as if the wind had brought Mr. Hill and Mr. Petion the scent of something sweet, like the smell of goat's blood to my mother's dogs.

Striding in from the living room, Uncle Martin beat Granny off the porch because she never actually left, never actually rose from her lawn chair. Visitors came to her.

Well, look who we have here. Uncle Martin was dressed for court, in his gray suit and starched white button-down shirt, leaving off, however, his peruke, for this transaction. He repeated himself, *Look who we have here.*

Hello, Uncle Martin. I exited the sedan, shook his extended hand.

From her chair, Granny yelled into the kitchen, *Valerie! Where is that tea? I told you they would be coming soon.*

Hello, Granny. It's good to see you. I walked to her chair, gave the obligatory kiss on the cheek, shoulder-hugged with as little contact as possible.

Hello, hello! Martin. Granny Pascal. Mr. Hill was easy, lithe; repeating my gestures with the enviable ease of the less invested. Mr. Petion silently following his friend's lead.

Uncle Martin began with the prodding. *I never thought any niece of mine would need an escort to visit Tours.*

Well, these are some surprising times, Martin. Mr. Hill blocked for me.

They certainly are, Granny added from her seat.

Valerie brought out a tray of tea, cream, sugar, and paper serviettes, making eye contact with no one. Returned to the kitchen at nearly a sprint.

I helped Granny and everyone to their cup, took mine last. We sat and looked toward the sea.

What's that? I pointed to the foundation and first floor of a building spanning Tour's cliff, strands of rebar stretching here and there.

Oh, it's those Australians. They're building a hotel, Uncle Martin answered, apparently as eager as I was to talk about plans other than the one at hand.

Granny, it will block your view of the cove. I felt a need to state the obvious.

She sipped her tea.

Yes, well. That will take some time to finish. They underestimated the cost of the infrastructure. Uncle Martin was liberal with confidential information. The Australians were clients of Uncle George.

They didn't anticipate the depth they'd need to drill to anchor properly in the bedrock. Construction is at a halt until they find new investors.

You've developed quite an interest in my land recently, Jean. Granny's throat no longer too dry to speak.

Now you're talking about Godwyn, quick to respond. *It's my mom's interest, Granny. She's put a lot of work into it.* That day I looked like politics; surprised us all.

Uncle Martin piped up, *Your mother has never been wise when it comes to land, Jean. She puts her whole self into other people's property. This is just like what she did in California with that man, Harold.*

No small tremor, my anger shifted big as an earthquake along its fault.

Messrs. Hill and Petion sat, sipped tea, awaited their turn unruffled.

That is not the case and you know it, Uncle Martin. What do you and Uncle Charles need with another house anyway? Don't you have enough, you have to bully my mom out of hers?

In my mind, I borrowed my mom's cutlass, aimed for Uncle Martin's jugular, swung with all my might. Followed through. Blood boiling, I rose, left the porch to use the bathroom, told them, *I'll be right back.*

On the dining room wall I passed a photograph of my grandfather, and one of my mother that Grampy must have paid for, black and white and gray, yellowing from so much exposure to air over time, one long crease down the middle, accidentally bent long ago. I've passed that picture of her a hundred times, but that time I finally saw.

The length of her dress was white lace, embroidered outlines of flowers linked the fabric together, a sash of something resembling silk, a dried flower bouquet. Her arms bent to hold the flowers in their crook, poised in the position someone had placed her, double shadow on the curtain behind from the photographer's two standing lights. The carpet beneath her feet resembled the one in our old Victorian.

The length of her dress was what I noticed last but mentioned first, because it was easiest. The hardest was my mother's face, seventeen or so, exactly like mine, even tilted in the way I carry my head to this day, slightly forward, stooped somewhere between a request for permission and an apology, her neck long and thin. I never knew I had my mother's smile.

I'd never seen her real teeth. Ever since I can remember they've been false. In the photograph, her face had not yet let them go and they stuck through her thick wide lips, teeth too large for her small mouth, making her look gangly, like a child playing grownup.

I opened the bathroom door, sat on the toilet where Uncle George spent an entire night when he was sick because the women couldn't lift him back to his bed, Uncle Martin stuck in Bato due to bad weather.

The morning's winds had picked up, whistled through the house high-pitched. I didn't hear their raised voices until I stepped back onto the porch.

I smelled blood, and it wasn't mine. Mr. Hill was taking his turn, wiped his lips dry. *You know I could take this scandal island-wide by the evening news. To Nassau by noon tomorrow. Think of all those arrogant Americans laughing at our backward little nation, our banana republic. George Pascal the butt of their jokes. You know I'll do it, Martin. Everyone has suspected it since my brother's heart attack, and this is key evidence.* He threatened my uncle, not Granny, sitting silent, tea in lap, staring out past the half-built hotel, through her half-left view of Tours Cove and the sea.

Uncle Martin was uncharacteristically quiet, arms folded across his chest. Mr. Hill continued, pointing to the old Toyota parked in front, next to my grandmother's arching coconut tree,

Everyone knows that's George's car. Everyone. Mr. Williams saw Archie in the backseat the same day of his heart attack, two of George's Liberty men up front. The idiots left George's Toyota at my brother's house, Martin! They sent Mr. Williams to retrieve it the next day. He's had it ever since. George was sick, Martin. His double-faced men thought they'd be attending two state funerals that weekend; so why not pin the Prime Minister's death on George's cold body lying next to him?

I stood still at the threshold of the porch.

Hill reloaded. *George's own party was going to accuse him of killing Archie. They'd sold him out, expecting them to die together. But George's death took too long; all that damn organic food these women were feeding him, their fresh-squeezed juices. And by the time George passed, it didn't matter whether my brother's heart attack was natural or intended. Archie was long dead. His successor less of a thorn in Liberty's side . . . But then again, na. Who's to say George didn't organize the whole thing from right here on this porch? It was only his movement down at that point, not his mind.*

Idle threats, Leonard. But Uncle Martin's words lacked a necessary conviction.

We will not have George's name dragged through the mud. Granny spoke to her cove, invited a bargain.

What is it you want, Leonard? Uncle Martin sneered. *Hasn't your family eaten their fill of ours as yet?*

Mr. Hill lost his detachment, and I realized mine wasn't the only blood boiling. Together we were a volcano, ready to explode.

Perhaps Mr. Petion could read his friend even better than I could, because he rose from his tea to suit the occasion of his cue, spoke to Granny politely as a little boy. *Granny Pascal. An old bachelor like myself always appreciates a good cup of tea. Thank you very much for having us.* He stood firm. *We know how important George's memory is to you . . .*

Granny wet her lips with milky tea, said to her saucer, *I am an old woman, Mr. Petion, with few things left that are dear to me. My son was very important to this island, as was his father. I have always supported them, and that does not end with their deaths. The house is not important to me anymore. Sophie can have it.* Then, to the half-built hotel blocking her cove, *Good day, gentlemen.*

The four of us, children, obeyed. Uncle Martin took Granny's teacup for her; Messrs. Hill and Petion nodded and turned to the car; I went to her side, pecked her stiff, cold cheek.

The drive home largely silent, they dropped me off at Godwyn, left my uncle's Toyota next to the barren plum tree out front, continued toward Bato, carried on with the rest of their morning.

Fatima, busy in the kitchen cooking something for dinner, hadn't fed the dogs yet. She'd sooner let them starve. She really hated them.

No leftovers to add to their bowls, I gave them dry kibble, filled their water bowl, heard them come running from, undoubtedly, someplace they shouldn't have been.

My mother was still sleeping.

Except for Fatima in the kitchen, I was alone. My family's blood on my hands, I felt like a traitor; like I'd burned every bridge to belonging anywhere. Uncle Martin and Granny hated me even more than they did after I'd merely spread their family name in mud, rolling out back with Susan. This time I'd gone too far, taken their hallowed ground, given it to my mother.

And had I really even gone there for her? Or had I gone for myself? Me, too scared to even commit her to my firm's medical insurance for fear of having a full dependent. Was it she who couldn't afford to lose another home, bringing me to Baobique? Or was it me, running there on my own to press a desperate finger against a burgeoning leak, my mother and I a cracked dam if I'd ever seen one.

Uncle George's Toyota, engine still warm from the trip to Tours, was just across from his grave, next to his father's. In a couple steps I was at the side of Grampy's cement marker, his epitaph, *All for One and One for All,* weathered down from the years. Next to him, Uncle George's marble gravestone more expansive, his words cryptic only to outsiders: *CarCom to CarCom.*

It is hard to imagine who I would have become if my mother had never left Baobique for the States, if I would have been more like the Hills or the Pascals. I know my blood is Baobiquen, but every time I go there I want to slit my wrists, drain it out of me— every drop.

I came out to my mother when I was twenty-two, at the intersection of Van Ness and Market—one of the busiest in downtown San Francisco. At the time, it seemed like as good a place as any. Looking back, I might have waited until she'd completed her left-hand turn.

I guess it didn't occur to me that the news I was gay would be as distracting to her as it was to me.

We were on our way to dinner at a Mexican restaurant whose taco salad with the lettuce bowl my mom liked so much, a precursor to her subsequent attempts at edible landscaping at Godwyn—her purple cabbages always winding up in some pot of soup or another down the road in Sommerset.

We stayed in the intersection long past our green arrow, a line of angry drivers growing behind us as I coached her through the necessary acceleration, and then off to the side of the road.

I apologized for my reckless timing and we made a pact not to mention the matter again until we got to the restaurant. After our flan, my mom looked at me and told me to *be careful,* not to mention what I'd told her in the car to anyone until after I'd been accepted to law school, told me not to jeopardize my plans over something like this.

Except for my confirmation that, *no*, I was not actually sleeping with anyone at the time, that was all she asked, all I answered. But later on, distracted in the parking lot, not remembering where she'd parked, I heard her say, not to me really, more to herself; she said, *I could never have told Mama that.*

Chapter 17

MY MOTHER MIGHT NOT HAVE shown me how to live my life, maneuver its twists and turns or weather its storms, by being, herself, a shining example of grace. And perhaps I could learn to forgive her for that.

But the lack of her touch was less troublesome to me than the lack of my own back.

There was something about Susan that never felt quite right, something threatening I couldn't quite place my finger on. Maybe it was because that threat was inside me, not her. And I'd been looking at the wrong person.

It's easy enough to say I was not loved the way I needed, but not that it left me unable to love in return; harder to admit I'd lost faith in the idea that my body could have melted to someone's touch; so stiff had I become from sitting frozen to my spot at the tops and bottoms of those stairwells to which I had followed my mother. Waiting. Watching.

It seems to me there are two types of mistakes. There are those you pay for all at once, like a fine or a traffic ticket, and there are those mistakes you pay for little by little, over time, like walking away from someone you shouldn't, coming home Monday, Tuesday, Wednesday, alone to the same bare walls and the cumulative harm repetition brings.

I don't know exactly which part of me never wrote back to Susan. But it was a part of me that, like my mother when I was just a child, crawled into her bed after work every day and stayed there for years.

Some things you don't get over for a long time: You can say goodbye, fly thousands of miles, pass month after month, all without really moving forward.

The things that make you stick in time to this spot or that can take years. Or they can happen in an instant.

I don't consciously think much about the day my Uncle Martin found Susan and me making love on the cliffs at Godwyn, about the bulge in his pants and the hatred in his voice stopping me cold in my tracks, gasping for air, searching shaky ground for some semblance of cover.

I don't think much about the letters I received, like clockwork, every week from Susan after we left Baobique, asking me *how on God's green earth* I could hide from her. Yet I pictured her asking me those questions as I read each and every one of the letters, her surgeon's hands grasping the air in front of her, trying to stitch our severed pieces back together—the only constant at the end of that grasp, the emptiness of a fist closing in on itself.

It was that last letter that got me. Startled me into panic. When Susan said she'd come to the States, I didn't know what to do. No one had ever just handed themselves to me that way before.

And I wasn't ready. It was as if I'd been nodding off at the top of the stairs and my mother had risen, washed her face in the porcelain sink next to her bed, opened the door to the master bedroom, and gleefully asked me what I wanted for dinner.

Susan's letter came to me like that, an offer I was simply not prepared to accept.

Standing outside Godwyn's shelter, like Granny's big copper to catch the rain, I dreaded going in to my mother, felt as if I was leaving the storm just to enter its eye.

Inside the house, Fatima had finished the chicken and rice, grated enough soursop into juice to fill two pitchers: one for the fridge, one for the freezer. She wrapped up her things in a crinkly plastic bag and started down the drive before waving goodbye— maybe so I couldn't find something else for her to do before she went. Like me, she didn't seem to mind the rain; took her sandals in her hand.

That left just me, my sleeping mother, and Uncle George and Grampy come in from the weather. The four of us, a cacophony in my head I wished would hush.

Shhhhhhhh. The rain agreed.

Something to do would help. I still had Cynthia's hearing to try as soon as I returned to California; the continuance was only good until then. So I searched around for a nubby pencil, a couple sheets of loose paper, and worked on my opening statement— to soften the head of the hammer the new appellate decision just placed in my client's hand:

> *It is not easy to live right. It is not easy to be a mother. Like most of us, Cynthia was not given a blueprint with which to raise her daughter. She does not have an agenda. She does, however, have a biological and, at this point in time, a legal right to Sadie that Linda does not.*
>
> *And while life is not usually as simple as that, this case is.*

Would that it wasn't, though. Would that I could have argued Linda's side instead of Cynthia's.

> *Family. There are many things that symbolize it. But let's take just one. Home.*

Their house having signified home for Linda, Cynthia, and Sadie for the past four years. 5050 Great Highway, San Francisco. Their very own house. Bought with their very own savings. Painted, mowed, cleaned, repaired with their very own hands. Kept dry with a $50 sump pump, two garden hoses, a screwdriver, and four-hour checks, 'round the clock, to keep the rainwater from rising to the top of the crawl space under Sadie's room and coming inside. Their house. Home to two grown women, one small child, and one slightly overweight corgi, all of whom felt safe inside since their first night of arrival, in the cold of February with both heaters broken and a fireplace unsafe to use. Family. With a backyard brown from the sun nine months out of twelve, except for the bright green path directly above the leaky sewage pipe, upon which grows the healthiest grass in the neighborhood. Home. At the edge of Golden Gate Park and above what was once the shifting water of the Pacific. Land reclaimed.

Up until three weeks ago, Linda was, legally, Sadie's second mother. And she did what mothers do: She put a roof over her daughter's head; she put food in her daughter's stomach; she kept her warm and dry in winter. Today, Linda continues to do what family does for family. Fight.

This one, though, is a losing battle. The courts have spoken.

Soon, I would likely win my first real case. And I wished I wouldn't.

Like it or not, I had a responsibility to my client. Just as, like it or not, I had a responsibility to my mom. But those mantles others saw on me, of daughter and attorney, I did not wear comfortably. All this speaking for others had me losing my own voice.

Chapter 18

S O IT IS TRUE. YOU DO EXIST.

Susan's voice, crisp and direct, called me back. And instantly I was in Baobique again. My heart raced.

She continued, linen skirt in bold batik, walking firmly as her words, *I'd heard the U.S. Postal Service hadn't disbanded. The only other possibility I could think of for so many unanswered letters was that you'd passed on. Like your uncle. Or maybe you were a ghost all along, a figment of my overactive imagination.*

I let her swing away, held still for all she had. I deserved it. Didn't answer. I waited with my eyes on her espadrilles.

She'd cut her hair short against the heat; black wire-rimmed glasses framed her green eyes.

But I couldn't look her in the face, for fear she'd see through to something I wasn't ready to show.

And she, not vindictive, changed the subject for me all on her own. Softened, *I hear your mummy is not well. I've come to check on her.*

I rose from my paper at the dining room table—let lie my future argument, etched thick in lead, put down my mother's pencil, and brought Susan to her room. *Thank you*, was all I could say.

In her bedroom, my mom was as I'd left her the night before, naked under the cotton sheet, so flat and motionless she could have been dead. But wasn't. I could see her chest rising, falling, rising, falling, to some slow internal clock.

Susan took her side, moved mechanically, unencumbered by the years that this image took me back, seeing my mom in bed again while the world swirled in chaos outside cedar planks, nearly rotted through.

I stuck close to the perimeter of the bedroom, only there to answer questions when asked.

Has she ever been like this before?

I stared blank at the bed, then right to closed shutters.

Susan's were not the first letters to which I'd withheld a reply. Once or twice a semester in college, my mom would write me. Her scrawl, legible to only the two of us—lines and lines I never read. I would take her letters from my mailbox in the student union, hide them deep under the books in my backpack, then pile them up at the back of my sock drawer as soon as I returned to my dorm.

How could I tell Susan, *Yes, she slept through my entire childhood. Can't you see the scars?* I couldn't. And that's not what she meant anyway. So I told Dr. Hill the truth: *Yes. For some years, when I was young, she had long spells like this.* Hoped she could help.

We are not as quick to medicate for a major depression in Baobique as they are in the States. Supplies are expensive. So I think we should wait a bit and see if she comes out of it on her own.

Voicing statements that sent me crashing, without even a hint of apology for what she'd just said about my mother, Susan moved to the shutter, turned its creaky wooden handle counterclockwise, and threw it open.

Defensive at her nonchalance, I pushed back, *My mother's not that depressed.*

Susan looked at me like I was a complete idiot, left the bedroom. Me, standing in the middle of it, staring at my mother's flaccid face.

Sharp and too-loud behind thinning walls, the telephone rang analog from the dining room bureau and scared me from my spot.

I hated talking to people there, but Susan was a guest, so I was the only one to answer. Unfortunately, Fatima'd remembered to remove the receiver's lock.

I picked up to my uncle, CarCom to CarCom. *Jean, this is Martin. Granny is ill. Is Susan at Godwyn? I just spoke with Leonard and he said she went to check on Sophie.* His voice breathy with alarm.

Oh my God. What's wrong with Granny?

Where's Susan?! he yelled, but not at me. A boy, Uncle Martin teetered toward tears.

From across the bureau, Susan had heard, heeded my tone, took the receiver from my outstretched hand. She listened to my screaming uncle, unruffled.

It took us some time to move my mom to the backseat of Susan's Subaru. She used smelling salts to wake her. We dressed her in practical clothes: sweat pants and rubber gardening boots.

Sometimes it took a whip, sometimes a carrot, to keep my mom moving. But for Granny it took the strength to hold that whip, that carrot, out in front of my mom. Trouble followed when she lost her grip.

Gain title! Gain title! That's all my mom was ever thinking about. Her world manageable, maybe, only one thought at a time. Everything else, just too much.

But things were changing by the minute. Her eyes mostly closed, right then it was up to me to see it all; adjust accordingly.

Ever since I'd known Granny, all she'd ever done was sit on that porch of hers, tell us all what to do. Up until that morning, with Mr. Hill and his threats about Uncle George.

Susan pulled us up to Granny's wrought iron gate, cut the engine, and, before I had time to even turn to the backseat, was halfway inside Tours' cement walls, sea blast chipping away. Susan with Granny, left me with my mom. I went to her grudgingly, like I'd pulled the short end of the stick for that particular event; unbuckled her; patted tiny slaps on her cheeks to bring her to.

Charles will be here by tomorrow morning. Uncle Martin, not two inches from Susan's heels, as my mom and I approached.

Through Granny's bedroom door, opening onto her front porch, I could see her lying there. Motionless as my mother would have liked to be, if I wasn't underneath her left armpit, dragging her into the second bedroom.

Before laying her down, I pulled off her rubber boots. After, covered her, clothed in soft cotton. Her tight curls flat with sweat against her forehead.

That morning, a sea change, everyone lying down by afternoon.

It seemed, sometimes, the way they carried on, at each other's throats at every second, there was no love lost between my mom and Granny.

I knew my mom felt closer to Auntie Lillian, all the way in England, than she did to Granny, just across the hall. Auntie Lil took my mom in some, during second form, after Granny'd given up on enforcing her futile One-Mile walks and started regarding my mom more and more with disgust and dismissal.

Jean, Susan broke my reverie, *I'm going back to the hospital. I have rounds to do. You should stay near your granny, she is not well at all.*

Will she be all right? I whispered. Some things should not be voiced so loudly.

I don't think so, Jean. She's had a heart attack. And she's very weak, Susan said softly, with a sad smile. *Despite her iron fist, your grandmother is ninety-five years old. She cannot hold on to you all forever.*

Should we take her to the hospital?

It's up to you all. Martin thinks she wouldn't want to go. And there's not so much more we could do there for her. We're already over-capacity.

I started to panic. *But we should do something!*

You are doing something. You came here to be with her. You cannot stop time itself, J.

Uncle Martin was outside on his cell phone talking, I think, to Uncle Charles.

My breath was hard, like the weight I was carrying had just doubled.

Susan assured me before she left that she'd be back directly after rounds at Grampy's hospital, then too full for Granny, and left me alone with my family.

The wind outside strong, strong.

I moved from my mother's side to my grandmother's, pulled in a lawn chair from her front porch, placed it on the urine-stained carpet beside her bed, the same bed from which my mom and Auntie Clara last year failed to lift Uncle George in time for the toilet late one night—leaving his mark.

Granny lay there, weak, in a bed steeped in death, looking at the ceiling—the only thing moving, her eyelids for the blink—perhaps waiting for Grampy to come get her in his old black motorcar, drive her away to a new home yet again.

Uncle Martin, frantic on his cell phone, prepared to leave in his Four-Runner, pointed directly to me as if he was singling me out to make a 911 call, told me, *Jean, stay with Granny today. I'll be back this evening.* Zoomed off through Granny's imaginary boundary.

Auntie Clara in her own house, out back; Valerie in the kitchen; my mom across the hall in an altered state; it was just me and Granny.

Nothing to do but sit. I stared through wrought iron, past standing strands of Australian rebar, to the sea and its low horizon with the day's stormy clouds. Everything swirled: the trees, the mountains, the sea. Looking out, a tiny piece of me was glad I wasn't flying in right then and was already there with my two feet on that slippery ground. At least I didn't have as far to fall; the worst that could happen, a few bruises here and there.

But it was too hard to sit still. And Granny wouldn't want respectable visitors to see her that way. So, I took the toenail clippers from her dresser and one by one clipped off the curly gray whiskers growing from her chin and upper lip as she breathed and blinked, breathed and blinked.

From Granny's clotheslines, behind the kitchen, Valerie explained that *de wind is pushin' de rain away.* No one knew how she did it, got Uncle Martin's shirts for court so white, down there by the river with a hard brick of detergent. But only the men were allowed to tell her. *I don't know how you do it, girl,* Uncle Martin would say when he dressed for morning hearings, there, up north at Granny's, even though Valerie was just as old as he was.

The clothes, on lines between a frangipani and a cedar, clipped to the rope like tethered birds.

As women, though, we couldn't comment because even though she really was, Valerie wasn't allowed to be better than us at anything. My mom preferred her Maytag, took the last of the money from her settlement with Harold and shipped it out in a big plastic container along with her jeep, her green gardening rubbers, and her Wolfe range.

My mom had told me she could see when Uncle George was

about to pass—some slight flash of panic, a few extra breaths of this world's air. She'd taken his hand and squeezed it, put her other arm around the back of his neck, pressed her cheek to the top of his high forehead, told him over and over: *Let go, George. Let go.* Against his struggle to stay.

I didn't do it on purpose, exactly, but I let go Granny's hand because Auntie Clara came in dressed for church and said she was off to some big Methodist service in Tete Queue, Granny's home township. I needed to get out. So I left Granny alone with Valerie in the kitchen; left her and my mom to fight out their silent battle over Godwyn, deep in sleep on opposite sides of the hall.

Auntie Clara drove.

On the way to the church, we passed a cement foundation that was supposed to have been an elementary school, stopped beside it for a view of the sea. The building was started by Uncle George's party before the last election. But then Hill's party beat them out and blocked construction because of spite.

There was no reason Granny was a Methodist other than the fact that she'd always been one. Same with my mom and Auntie Clara.

When we got there, I was introduced to people I would not remember under the host congregation's octagonal gazebo at the top of a hill on the side of a mountain, overlooking the sea. Outside, two flamboyant trees bursting orange. Their statement, perhaps, against the monotony of the event.

The service was a big one, made up of all the island's circuits. We sat by congregation. Auntie Clara and I had to squeeze between a mother and daughter who used to work for her, cleaning and washing laundry, until the mother walked off with six yards of paisley fabric my cousin had sent down from Florida. They framed us in matching paisley dresses. Auntie Clara proclaimed she had never seen anything so bold, such *brass face*. But what could she do? She was in church.

Each congregation took a turn standing, singing a hymn of its own choosing. There were a total of eight congregations. Auntie Clara complained about the length of the service, started counting the number of each group's verses. Said to a woman in front of her, *But these are too long. They've ten!*

I stared out the hole in the wall closest to me, signifying a window, felt the breeze on my face, my neck; looked toward the sea. I wasn't quite sure if I was glad I'd gone or whether I should've stayed by Granny's side. But maybe sometimes, when there's nothing to be done, simple motion isn't as meaningless as it feels.

The minister offered a middling sermon about the conversion of their religion's founding father on a street called Alder's Gate, in London. On the front of the handout printed up for the occasion, a Caucasian couple held a book of hymns. Around me, not a single white face in the crowd.

Chapter 19

MAYBE IT WAS GRAMPY, snuck into Auntie Clara's backseat, retracing his way back to life with us this time, come to get Granny; take her back.

Maybe there's a type of knowing that just can't be explained, because by the time we returned, I already knew, even as we pulled slowly up to the gate at Granny's front porch, up alongside Uncle Martin's car, and Susan's.

I jumped out of the car while Auntie Clara was still rolling it into position, ran inside to find Susan, arms folded, above Granny's stiff body, Granny's eyes still staring up at the ceiling, frozen in waiting. Her son at her side.

Auntie Clara followed me in, started to make noise.

I walked back out to the front porch to catch my breath away from her screeching, felt Susan's eyes follow me out.

Mr. H., a man who works my mother's garden, keeping away the underbrush with his machete, had been chopping away at the roots of one of her coconut trees. Ten years he'd been working for my mom. Ten years, little by little, he'd been chopping away at those roots. Earlier that week the tree finally toppled, just like that, in the last big storm.

I walked against the winds over to the coconut tree at the far end of Granny's front yard, the one next to the tall cedar. A sharp pain pierced the top of my head.

I woke to Susan's pocket light shining straight into my eye, her soft fingers callously stretching its lid open way too far.

Ow! I groaned. My entire head throbbed.

Never, ever, walk underneath a coconut tree, J! Coconuts fall all the time . . . But don't worry, na. We've killed the one that got you. It won't be troubling you anymore. She clicked off her light, let go my face, gave me a quick wink and an almost imperceptible smile.

I tried to get up, but the throbbing in my head held me down. All I could do was start to cry. So I did.

Susan took my face again in her hands, wiped the tears.

I tried to push her away. *Stop, they'll see us! They'll see us! We'll go to jail!*

But she didn't stop, bent her head down to mine. *Shush, J. It's all right . . . We're in the maid's quarters. Everyone is up front. They're busy with your granny right now. I told them I'd look after you.*

Susan, my head . . .

I know, J. I know. She showed me the towel, full of ice, she'd been holding to my scalp.

What happened? The panic lessened.

Just a coconut. It fell on your head. She smiled, stifled a laugh.

A coconut fell on my head? Are you joking?

No, J.

That's ridiculous. I started to laugh, but the movement was a bad idea. *Ow!*

You should sit up now, if you can. I've already given you something for the pain. She slid an arm underneath my back, lifted me to sitting. *Scoot back against the wall.*

Susan? I whispered.

Yes, J, she followed.

Granny's dead.

She took my hand in hers, squeezed. *Yes. I know.*

Susan?

Yes, J.

It's my fault.

She smiled, small. *Silly girl, it was life alone that killed your granny. But you do have very bad timing.*

Susan, I was crying again, still whispering, *don't leave.*

I'm not going anywhere, J.

Susan?

Yes, J.

Why am I crying? I can't stop.

You tell me, J . . . You tell me. But she pulled out her pocket light again, checked my pupils.

Out back, always, the wind through the trees.

Out front, voices, baritone and soprano. All running together. One of them, my mother's.

Chapter 20

GRANNY'D ALWAYS SAID she wanted to be buried in Tete Queue next to her mother, the wash girl, not at Godwyn next to Grampy. But no one mentioned that right then. Mostly, she said it for attention. Mostly, when Granny talked, it wasn't for conversation, it was just to hear someone answer her back, just to know that someone, anyone, was still around.

Susan told me I was not to sleep tonight, for fear of slipping into a place from which I could not wake. Like Granny. Uncle George. Grampy.

There was noise out front. The pain medication was taking effect, and I was curious to hear what the others were discussing so loudly on the evening of their mother's death, a time, I would have thought, for gentle reflection. So I moved slowly from Susan's side in the maid's quarters to join my uncles, my aunts, my mother, scattered wide—a winter constellation—across the front porch, under the electric light of a single bulb hanging from the ceiling, collecting mosquitoes.

Susan followed me as far as the living room, did not enter my family's circle. She lay down on the couch. Rested.

Although I had arrived mid-discussion with a lump still swelling on top of my head, even a child could tell something more than just Granny was going on. My mom stood on wobbly legs between her brother and Granny's iron gate, locked this time of evening from outsiders come to intrude; sea blast palpable in the strong winds against her back—once again in danger of imminent collapse.

I deflected their attention from her to me, held the doorway, though, for support against the hot throbbing in my head and the chill of their reception. But I had lost my ability to be polite. I hurt and was sick of all the endless argument.

What?! I yelled, deep with all the authority I could find. *What now?*

Uncle Martin asserted his spin: *The family will have to reevaluate Godwyn, in light of Granny's passing.*

What do you mean, reevaluate? I could see his backpedaling a mile away.

Susan intervened. I hadn't seen her get up, join me in the doorway, but there she was. She placed a steadying hand just above the small of my back, said to my uncle, *This cannot be resolved tonight. You all should be ashamed of yourselves for even discussing it.*

My head was spinning: Granny's moon appeared and disappeared behind fast-moving clouds; mosquitoes circled the electric bulb. I was not steady.

Susan took my arm, led me to her car, and buckled me in, but not before my stomach heaved and I got sick all over Granny's imaginary garden. Susan repeated the process with my mother, and drove us to Godwyn.

You cannot sleep tonight, she reminded me, after seeing my mom to bed, feeding the dogs, and locking Rascal inside with us. That was the way to do it: one dog outside, one in, for security.

But I was tired. I told her so, and she was unsympathetic,

decided we'd make ginger beer to keep me this side of slumber.

Until my mom moved back to Baobique, I never knew there was such a thing as ginger beer. She'd known the recipe by heart since she was a child, but apparently forgot to tell me about it. Ever.

It is, simply, root beer, but made from ginger. So it's sharper, has more of a bite.

Susan filled the biggest pot we could find with water from the faucet, placed it to boil on the Wolfe range while I stood at the counter grating the ginger Fatima had rooted up sometime the week before.

The beer is stronger if you grate the root.

You like it too sweet, J. That's not how it's supposed to taste, Susan warned me, when it came time to add the sugar and I measured out an entire cup.

I know. Don't ruin the whole batch. Let's just take some out for me and I'll sweeten it myself.

But this is ginger beer. What you want is some child's drink. She poured two glasses, tall and obstinate with too little sugar, over ice.

Blame my mother for giving me her sweet tooth. But she makes it with extra.

Exactly. She's lived away too long. I'm showing you how it's really done. What do you think your mother knows about making ginger beer, na? All you Pascals take a sip of water and claim you've discovered the river.

She took the pot of beer from the stove. Poured the entire batch into three standing bottles, capped them tight from air and such.

You are just like your family. You come to Baobique for a few weeks out of your life and tell me how to make ginger beer. It is arrogance through and through.

We were not really arguing about beer; my head was hurting and I felt, yet again, on the edge of tears.

Susan moved to the dining room table, to her left a hole in the cedar floorboards above the crawlspace under the house where Lucia slept; above her head, bats in the attic hidden only by the thinnest veneer.

She finished, *I hate to see them in you* . . . Then started again. *You expect things to come to you, J. Rest themselves at your feet without any effort on your part. But it's you that has to take a step or two if you want something, na.*

I wanted, more than anything, to go back to that afternoon, when she was just being nice, just taking care of me; or farther, to those nights she'd crawled on top of me of her own free will and her skin shone back brown against the light from all those stars. But between us, things were not so easy as simple touch anymore.

I wanted to kiss her, but instead I apologized. *Susan, I'm sorry I never answered your letters.*

An entire year, Jean. An entire year I had no one to talk to after what happened.

I'm sorry.

I left my home. Why do you think I took that residency in Nassau? I had to leave Baobique! I didn't think I could come back, your uncles made such noise. And all that time, all that time, na, I was still willing to believe you were worth it . . . *And stupidly, when my father told me you were here again, to see about your mummy's house, a little piece of me was waiting for you to come running to my door, convince me all over again that we have something—you and I.*

Susan, we do. I'm sorry.

That is the first accurate statement you've made all day: You are sorry!

Can we never be that close again? I asked, softly as possible.

Her silence steamed like a tea kettle—no one watching, save

maybe Grampy and Uncle George, my mother sleeping behind closed doors.

I held still, on some verge.

Susan kept her gaze off mine, but gave a little. *Perhaps ours was a false start, Jean.*

What's this, then? Another? I was tentative, where Susan wasn't.

No. This one here is the real race. If you want me, J, it's your step forward.

I stepped. *I want to touch you.*

Then touch me.

It was dark in the guest bedroom, the shutters closed tight, tight, to keep us safe from intruders, or weather, come knocking. But the wind, strong against the broken boards of the house outside, made me wonder if we weren't missing signals Grampy and Uncle George might have been trying to send.

Inside the guestroom, Susan lit a citronella candle for the mosquitoes, unknotted the netting to cascade around the bed, whispered, *At the hospital, I can always tell the foreign-born children from their mosquito bites.* It was too dark to tell if she was smiling or not.

The net was torn. If the mosquitoes wanted to get me, they would. That's just the way it is for me there.

Inside our tent of ghostly white mosquito netting, its edges tucked tight around the four corners of the mattress, Susan promised, *I'll rub your skin with aloe in the morning to stop the scars from taking hold.*

Every inch, I told her, finally. *I want every inch of you.*

It's just that there was something about Susan; some spark ignited, knowing beforehand that when she touched my arm, my leg, my back, gripped tight and pulled herself to me, she was entering a place already familiar, a person built on volcanoes, red clay, and salt. It was a comfort I had felt with no one else that this woman knew trails inside me I could never have found alone.

I didn't become a Pascal, it seemed, until I reached adulthood. And then, all at once, it happened. I looked in a mirror, doubled-up in some department store, and all over my back—Grampy's moles. Mostly I pretended they weren't there. But Susan laughed, our eyes grown accustomed to the dark, she connected the dots, lightly with the very tip of her long, thin finger—sending pictures from her head to my skin, lining me with her touch. And apparently, I wouldn't have given them up for anything, those thousand and three moles, from my shoulders to the lowest arch of my back.

Silently, I thanked the ceiling, Grampy swirling around somewhere up there, looking down on Susan and me, wearing his skin—marked for eternity.

Chapter 21

ORNING BROKE CLEAR AND WIDE.
I was not supposed to sleep, but I woke to the sound of birds just this side of the open window, and to Susan's soft fingers gently separating my eyelids to get at my pupils.

I wasn't to let you sleep. She looked a bit concerned, disappointed in herself for failing me in that way. *But it looks as if you've made it through.*

My head only hurt to the touch. I leaned it against her, not wanting to start the day.

I've got early rounds, J. And you and your mummy should get back to Tours.

I moaned in forced agreement. She was up, and right. The sun had risen whether I liked it or not, inching higher and higher in the sky; and there were matters to which I needed to turn my attention.

Susan leaned down to me one last time, barely graced the top of my forehead with her lips, and smiled. *She's up this morning, J. She's made breakfast.*

What? I was slow, still a bit groggy.

But Susan was already out the door, called back to my mom, *Goodbye, Mrs. Souza. You take it slow today, na. Doctor's orders.*

I heard noise from the dining room, rose to investigate: plates to wood, silverware, glasses with fresh juice.

The redness in her eyes had cleared and Susan was right, my mom *was* up—moving, actually, a little too fast for my achy head.

You're up, I observed flatly, as I sat down at the table in front of one of the two place settings, poured myself a cup of tea, its tannins golden brown, spreading their color to fill the space of my mug. I sipped. Took a few bites of egg in the welcomed silence. Early-morning birds outside the open door.

But my mom didn't want to be peaceful. She was up. And angry. Started right in on me. *Jean, I want to talk to you about Godwyn before we go to Tours today.*

The egg in my stomach wound itself into a knot, swelled to twice its natural size, impinged on my lungs.

Mom! Please! Can't I at least finish breakfast in peace? She was either on or off those days. I couldn't take it much longer. But by then I didn't want peace either. Nor eggs. So I let her have it: *All this family ever does is fight. Fight. Fight. Fight. Nonstop, Mom. It's nonstop and I want off!*

My whole life, it seemed as if I never belonged to my mother's family, as if it had been a gift I had neglected to receive, forgotten on Christmas like those many Fridays waiting on the sill of the picture window for my dad to pick me up for the weekend in the Mustang that kept forgetting the way back to our house. Then, just when things started falling apart and the gift turned out to be rotten—like a guava left too long at the bottom of the tree, poked by worms and bugs and birds alike—her family turned into a curse. And I was first in line to catch its hell.

When Grampy died, his children had little experience with change so permanent as death. They left his body whole; laid it, thick, between sheets of cedar in a casket his boys had built themselves:

chopping and sanding and nailing the boards together so tight it would take a long, long time for anything to eat its way through, and by that time Grampy'd be safely in heaven.

They carried his casket on their backs all the way from Tours to the burial plot out back—shrouded in orchids and frangipani under a steady August shower—cutting in from the access road, uphill to his grave.

Thing is, Grampy never went to heaven at all. He stayed right there at Godwyn. Walked its rooms at night.

It's not like I expected Grampy's strong hand, or even Uncle George's, to reach down from the sky, grab me by the collar, and shake, shake, shake me to my senses. But they were in the trees, the floorboards, the salty film on my skin after a sea bath. I breathed them in the air, my lungs expanding, stretching skin marked with Grampy's moles.

I don't even believe in ghosts. But those were no ghosts: Grampy, Uncle George, Granny too. They were alive as any living voice—telling me things like who I was and why, and where I could belong should I simply say *yes*.

Even though they couldn't really kill me, they could—in an instant—blow out the flame that warmed my blood under the guise of a gentle evening breeze.

Just before midday we got the call from Tours: Uncle Charles had arrived. He wanted to settle matters with Godwyn before driving Granny's body down to Bato to be cremated. There'd be a lot to do to prepare for the funeral.

They had Valerie make the call.

I was a little unclear, though, about what they meant by *settling matters with Godwyn*. My mom and Granny held title as joint tenants, which meant when Granny passed, all ownership rights transferred directly to my mom. Uncle Charles, Uncle Martin, even Granny from her unfilled grave, had no say in the matter. Neither law nor logic supported their presumptions. They'd not been added as heirs to Granny's share, so my uncles' names were not on the deed.

I knew, though, that wouldn't stop them. I dreaded my role—playing counsel.

Chapter 22

AT TOURS THERE WAS A BUSTLE OF ACTIVITY. It was a good thing my mom was up, because even if I had remembered to stop by the police station for a temporary driver's license, the roads were more of a challenge than I was up for right then. We pulled up in the front yard, under the frangipani, its cascading white flowers. Uncle Martin's Four-Runner was crooked in front of the porch, the open gate.

We passed through the empty living room and made our way back to Valerie in the kitchen. Uncle Martin and Uncle Charles stood together, arms folded, beside Granny's big copper, full to the rim from last night's storm. I knew they'd heard the car, but they stayed rooted—made us wait.

Fine by me. The only danger, imminent idleness. There in Granny's kitchen, though, my mom was right at home, took up the one good knife and started chopping things. Valerie took pity on me, handed me an empty pot, asked me to return it to the Australians living in the trailer just around the bend, Polly and Eugene of the half-built hotel.

Polly had sent up a pot of beans after hearing about Granny, to help with the company sure to follow. No one had thanked her as yet. The beans went bad overnight, left out. But I wouldn't tell her that. The first words I would utter to the stranger who lived across from Tours, one of the few but growing number of whites settling in Baobique, would be a lie. I would tell her we all enjoyed the beans very much.

Out on the road I passed a slow walker with a machete, exchanged only stares.

I didn't know Polly or Eugene's last name, but there was a truck with a *Koala Construction* decal on its side, on the tarish next to their trailer.

Their dog, a purebred ridgeback, announced my arrival before I called out, *Hello, hello*, and walked up to their little porch area.

Eugene was sitting at a small table: a large, pale man in khaki shorts and a polo shirt, sweating profusely during the mildest part of the day, looking at some plans, architectural drawings.

Although farther away and inside the trailer, it was Polly who greeted me first, rushing out the door at a speed verging on desperation.

I told them I was Sophie's daughter, come to return their pot, the beans were delicious, *thank you very much.*

They would have offered me juice, fresh-squeezed, if they were my grandmother, my aunt, my mother. Accepting their glass of water, I prayed it had been boiled.

I sat with them on their porch, stared out past the edge of the cliff to Granny's blue sea. Looking away from the water to their faces, only when I absolutely had to, I did the minimum to maintain my welcome, frontloading all those things that would get them to excuse my rudeness and lack of interest: *I am an attorney. I live in San Francisco. I grew up in the States. No, I do not visit Baobique often. I came to visit with my grandmother before she passed.* But enough.

Eugene, a little more forthcoming than me, said they'd moved to Baobique a couple of years ago to do construction work. Koala Construction was his. He was doing relatively well. Their biggest project, a six-story hotel that was now only half-built, would be their home once it was finished. But, of course, I already knew that. When completed, their hotel would block the entire view of our cove from Tours. Polly would run it. They were hopeful that a new wave of white settlers, in need of housing, would give them everything they need, financially, to finish the hotel. They all went to Eugene to build their homes. It just worked that way there.

Polly got a bit more personal, although only about my family, not about herself. Living just around the corner from Tours, she saw a lot of things visitors like myself didn't know about. Now that Granny had passed, Polly worried about Clara, who, bless her soul, was always losing her house keys. I should really have a duplicate set for both Auntie Clara's house and Tours made while I was there and leave them with Polly.

Just the other day, Polly had gone over to visit Granny, found her alone, lying on the floor, unable to get up. Polly didn't have a key to unlock the iron gate and Auntie Clara was in town, so Polly sat outside the house talking to Granny, making sure she was okay, until Auntie Clara got back an hour or so later. Polly should really have a set of keys.

Returning to Tours the back way, through the kitchen, I mentioned the story to my mom. But she just laughed at the idea, said Polly wanted those keys so she could have access to Granny's rum, said Polly was an alcoholic. Polly's last name was Whitchell. Just remember the *witch*, Mom said.

They were waiting for me out on the front porch in the lawn chairs just this side of Granny's stiff body: Uncle Charles and Uncle Martin, the family's remaining patriarchs, new to the throne and still uncertain of its reach.

No one knows why, but the law says corpses are to be buried feet facing east. The logistics of the family's plot made it so Uncle

George's headstone lay at the wrong end of his body. At the funeral, Uncle Charles was quick to remind guests to pay their respects to the dirt at his brother's head, so Uncle George could hear.

I was avoiding them, back there in the kitchen. I did it very well. The only thing I did better in Baobique, actually, was obey. So I came when they called.

They called me, not my mom, to discuss the situation with her house. But she followed me as far as the living room, busied herself by stacking and restacking the silverware underneath the dish towel in the corner, close enough to hear our words.

With Uncle Martin, the lawyer, everything he says comes out like argument, awaits rebuttal. But with Uncle Charles, a physician like Grampy, like Susan, his words come out with an authority hard to question, as if straight from God's lips. I know this is schooled, wouldn't want my doctor second-guessing himself over something as important as my life. But still, it was unnerving.

When I was little, just after the divorce, before my mom sunk roots into her mattress, Uncle Charles brought us up to Canada for a long visit. He had a brand-new house in an area zoned for development, with a swimming pool and a two-car garage with a Jaguar inside. One evening he took me out on the front porch to look at all the land, empty of neighbors. He rested his hand on my shoulder like my dad would have, if my dad were Uncle Charles.

Look around you, Jean. Someday, all this land will be built up, with houses and schools and shops. All it takes is a little vision, a little foresight.

There is something about land to a Pascal, as if without it we've no ground.

I could see the wheels turning, turning inside his head. When he and George were little, they'd walk, hidden in the bush, through the piece of land upon which now sits the Australians' half-built hotel, to the end and its steep drop to the Atlantic. Their sights, nearly two hundred degrees. So they could see almost everything. Almost. And they knew they were rich, in beauty alone, to have so much. Even though that land wasn't Grampy's, Charles and George would take it upon themselves to tear down makeshift shelters built by squatters. Creating their own consensus, they worked from underneath its authority alone—called it law: taking someone else's home, fabricating entitlement.

I knew those men like my alter ego.

But Uncle Charles thought he knew more about law than he really did; he wasn't George.

He told me, like he'd looked at my tonsils and they had to come out, calmly awaiting my agreement, *Jean, your granny has just died. We will bury her at Godwyn, of course, next to Grampy.*

I knew that, agreed, *Of course.* But what was the catch?

Your Uncle Martin and I have been talking about Godwyn. And because it is becoming increasingly central to the family's needs, with the burial plot, it needs to remain a family house—as Grampy intended.

I'm not sure I understand what you mean. I wanted him to say it.

Now that the ice was broken, Uncle Martin chimed in, in terms I'd understand. *Title to Godwyn will go to all of us; not to your mother alone. It's not fair for her to get the entire house to herself.*

Uncle Charles: *You wouldn't keep us from our mother's grave, Jean. I'm sure of that.*

Of course not, Uncle Charles.

Good. It's settled, then. Martin will draw up the papers.

I was surprised my mom was staying out of it; I knew she'd heard. Maybe she just didn't understand what her brothers were trying to pull. But I did. And I didn't stay quiet.

The thing is, Uncle Charles, it's not me that's keeping anyone out of Godwyn. The family has always owned the burial plot. It doesn't belong to my mom. The house, though, and that land adjacent to the graves, does belong to her. With Granny's passing, the joint title they shared already transferred to my mom.

No! He didn't like my confidence. *I just told you. The title will remain with the family . . . Let me ask you, Jean, do you know what this family has meant to this island?*

It wasn't really a question. So I didn't respond. Anything I'd say, he'd attack.

Uncle Martin sat back, understanding, perhaps better than Uncle Charles, that this was an argument, not a diagnosis, and that we were at an impasse that would not be crossed from our current posture.

It was crazy. Granny barely cold under cotton sheets in the next room; our hands should have been clawing the earth, digging her grave. Uncle Charles was wrong. He and his swimming pool, his Jaguar in Canada. I would not let him claim my mother's only roof. He'd always thought her more buoyant than she really was.

My mom almost drowned when her brothers taught her to swim. She was seven. Granny wouldn't have any of her children being scared of things as essential to life as the sea and thought it was time my mom and Auntie Clara learned to make their way in the water.

Grampy told the boys to see to it.

So Uncle George, Uncle Charles, and Uncle Martin rowed the girls out to the middle of the bay down at Champagne, where the water is warmed by radiated heat and gasses from volcanic activity bubbling up from porous rock and loose sand. The bright red coral just beyond is a national treasure now, protected by one of Uncle George's laws, but back then merely a marker of an under-water drop so steep it's still to be measured.

Uncle Charles, calm as the surgeon he'd later become, told the girls they couldn't sink because the salt in the water would buoy their small bodies to the surface. Uncle Martin, having just learned the trick himself, told them, *Just look for the bubbles. Look for the bubbles. Follow them up*. Uncle George rowed and rowed.

My mom and Auntie Clara were scared, kept shouting, *Turn around! Turn around!*

But the boys dropped anchor. Threw them in. And the girls went down against a flow of bubbles.

Uncle Charles was going to count to one hundred and twenty. But he only made it to ninety before George and Martin dove in after them, pulling their sisters back to the boat from the sandy bottom, willing their apologies light as air to breathe the life back in through Mom and Auntie Clara's purple lips.

Sometimes he was simply wrong.

But we were both wrong to be warring right then. Uncle Martin reeled us in, but not without a jab of his own.

All right, gentlemen, he said, addressing us both, *we will continue with this later. Charles and I have arrangements to make for Granny's funeral.*

Chapter 23

I NEEDED SOME SPACE FROM MY UNCLES and I took it. I did not ask what I could do to help with the arrangements. And I didn't ask my mom if she'd drive us back to Godwyn; I told her.

Let's go, Mom. We're leaving now.

In the car she lost her reticence. I got an unsolicited earful and started to see.

This was how things came around.

You should have been there for George's funeral, Jean. You should have seen it. They wanted total control.

Who's "they," Mom? I had to direct her line of thinking if I was to get any useful information.

Charles! Martin! Who else?! They wanted to let people inside the house. My house! They said they couldn't ask Dame Devon to sit under a tent. But if I'd let her in, everyone would have started in. What do they take me for, na? A fool? I said no! I locked them all out. Her eyes weren't watching the road, they were watching the events of that afternoon: Dame Devon and Granny, come to pay their respects, pitched together under nothing but a tarp to protect themselves from the hot sun.

I reminded her where we were. *Mom, watch the road.* But I had to ask; didn't want to have heard what I just did. *You didn't let anyone in the house during Uncle George's funeral? No one at all?*

It's my house, Jean! They would have overrun it. There were hundreds of people.

What if they needed to use the bathroom, Mom?

The state brought in the portable toilets. They trampled a whole section of my crotons! Look! As we pulled up the drive, she pointed to the flattened area, overgrown with bush from so much recent rain.

My mother was out of control. *Loss*, I said.

What? she yelled back.

Nothing. We parked in the carport.

As if everyone in my family didn't already have a head start, all that loss was making them crazy, bringing me right along.

Uncle Charles wanted Godwyn back because what he really wanted he couldn't have: he wanted back his baby brother, whose cancer he couldn't take away, and his mother, who died while he was on his way home. He wanted his family back, but all that was left was rotting cedar and a small patch of dirt upon which to lay their bodies, face their feet east.

Maybe it was me who needed to dig in my heels, stop our downward slide.

Chapter 24

A T GODWYN WE WERE COOLED by intermittent showers, maybe reaching to Tours, maybe not. My mother disappeared again into the gardens. But I didn't give chase. I sat on the covered porch, watched the rain, listened to it come and go under corrugated tin.

The flamboyant. The baobab. The guava. The plum. And me. All of us rooted there, growing.

With two beeps for notice, Susan's muddy Subaru turned off the road and up the drive, parked under a cedar. Rising from my seat, I saw she was not alone. A tall, long-limbed man, with even longer dreds, exited opposite her. He was beaming, boyish, in jeans and a polo shirt.

Together, they walked along my mother's croton hedge, the Jacob's Coat, its two-toned leaves, soft and fuzzy, some more purple than green, some more green than purple. His hand resting lightly at the small of her back. Susan looked straight at me; smiled, too, but stiffly.

Hello, I greeted them cautiously, politely from the porch.

Jean, this is Marcus Greene. He's a freshman in the assembly and has practically kidnapped me to come meet you.

Hello, Jean. His voice was confident but not arrogant. He took his hand from Susan's back and reached out to me. We shook and he continued, *I was a great admirer of your Uncle George. I followed his political career quite closely. I was so sorry when he passed . . . I'm sorry, too, about your Granny. That is certainly a lot for one family to bear.*

Wonderful. I looked to Susan for an explanation.

Marcus came with me to George's funeral, she offered.

We all looked to the ground, away from each other, for a split second.

Fine. They were standing in my mother's yard, I had to say something. So I did. *It's nice to meet you, Marcus. I'm sorry for their deaths, as well . . . But I'm afraid I'm not like my uncle, politically, at all. I'm sure I'd disappoint you if you knew me.* I wasn't feeling friendly toward this man with his hands all over Susan.

He was not troubled by my tone, threw back his head and laughed. Clapped a couple of times to some funny joke only he'd understood. *I know, Jean. I know.*

I asked, *What's so funny?*

Marcus confided, *Jean, I admired your uncle's abilities, not his platform. He was much too conservative for the new Baobique.*

The new Baobique? I was curious.

Susan rolled her eyes, sighed. *Please, please! Don't get him started. I'm only on a lunch break. We just came to say hello, not to give O.O.F.I. speeches.*

O.O.F.I.? Still curious, but not just about politics. Mostly, I wanted to know why Marcus could touch her so easily, why she rolled her eyes at him like they were an old married couple, and why his smile was so big by her side.

The only explanation I got, though, was the politics. Marcus was a member of the island's newest party, Free Islands. Free Islands was grabbing at the reigns of control with new ideas of banding together with other small islands, gaining strength through numbers in the international arena as an organized political unit—O.O.F.I., they call themselves, the Organization of Free Islands.

It was getting increasingly difficult for the island to gain revenue with no land tax and the bulk of its workable soil still tied up in private estates, owned by just a handful of families, as if no time at all had passed since the Europeans left Baobique to run itself.

Marcus told me all of that in mock confidence, pretending to keep the secret from Susan, shielding her side of his mouth with his hand, bending in my direction.

Weed that I was, I was green with envy at their interplay.

I will see you later, Jean, Susan assured me, as she initiated their departure, pulled away.

Marcus waved his long arms, called to me out the window, *I hope she will let us meet again, Pascal!* Happy, like a man with the world at his feet.

Jean! Jean . . . come!

My mom was out back by Grampy's grave, where the cliff dropped, steep, to rocks and a salty sea, clearing space for Granny. Never mind her brothers' threats, the situation's volatility. I do believe, honestly, that my mother will never change; always planting herself before it's time.

But Susan was right when she'd laid it out for me the day before. It was time I stopped asking my mother to be someone other than herself; time I met her where she was, instead of where I kept wanting her to be.

She waved me over with her machete, past the star fruit tree, the cherry guava, the larger, grafted guava. I cut my ankle on a low-lying pineapple plant, its long serrated leaves like a bread knife on my skin, drawing that blood the mosquitoes drank like rum.

Come. I want you to see this—talking with her hands, even as she carried a cutlass; I gave her a wide berth.

What's that? I did not reprimand her for jumping the gun, working the land before we smoothed things out with Uncle Martin and Uncle Charles. I gave up easily, played her game.

She held up a plant the length of her arm.

What is it? I asked.

It's a sego palm. The oldest in the world, she explained.

Neat. Where'd you get it?

Fatima brought it up from Sommerset. From Pastor Christian's garden. God bless his soul. He lived there forty years and then the church moved him to Bato. He was getting so old. They couldn't risk him living in the country. But mark my words, that man will die without his garden.

My mom put the palm back down, began to dig a hole on the cliff side of the graves, just in back of the headstones at Grampy and Uncle George's feet. Hard to tell if she kept moving out of purpose or worry.

I've decided the sego is going to be my signature plant.

The way my mom deals with the possibility of losing everything is to put everything she has into it. I, on the other hand, am the cautious one. I never rely on anything that could possibly be taken away, turn left and right around holes, like the ones still left in me from her.

She continued, *When they grow, the trees will act as a windbreak to protect the graves and slow the erosion of the cliff.*

That day, I did it her way.

We finished with the palms hot and sweaty, went inside for a drink of whatever juice Fatima had cold—lime. At the dining room table, we talked between ourselves about private things, like land and greed, as if Fatima wasn't just in the next room or walking here and there between sentences.

Outside the open shutter, a hummingbird, iridescent green, at the flamboyant's bright orange flowers, high up in the tree. Inside with us, a small black bird with a red breast.

If I'd been worried for my mother since she'd showed up at the Oakland airport, bloodred eyes and too many bags, I wasn't anymore. Not so much. As long as she could keep that house—her whole self, the bodies of her father, her brother, soon maybe her mother, and now my own blood from the pineapple plant, in its earth, where she could always reach down, sink her fingers in its dirt, and grab hold for balance.

She only ever falls apart, completely, now and then. Remains in pieces sometimes longer, sometimes shorter. Like me, to a degree.

This is how things come around. Maybe it was no accident I'd become my mother's daughter and a lawyer like my uncles. Those days I saw them in me everywhere I turned; the way I avoided, attacked, avoided, attacked.

Whether I settled matters or not, I could get on a plane and go back home to a life as anonymous as I chose. But my mom was stuck there. She needed her family intact, which meant I did, too.

Chapter 25

Each step ripe with the possibility of both, it'd gotten hard to tell forward from back, right from wrong. But I stepped anyway.

Granny used to say she didn't want to be buried at Godwyn. But Granny was dead. Like Grampy and Uncle George. And her voice could no longer be heard by the people around her. She could say all she wanted, but the only one who'd hear her would be my mom, maybe, late at night in the house, as just another angry shutter banging in the wind.

Mom, we're giving them access. I said the words to her as they came into my head, clearly, as if the answer had been staring me in the face the whole time.

Her face curled to object above the lime juice, yet I didn't care. I put my foot down, cut her off before she could complain.

Look, I said, cold like a lawyer, *I can make this happen, and you can't. They need to be able to use the burial plot, Mom. Not even you can stop them. Your land surrounds it on all sides. Any judge would give them a road.*

She complained anyway. *But Charles is talking about taking the whole house. It's my house, Jean. Look what I've made of it. That's the only reason he wants it. It's pure greed.*

Mom. Stop. Uncle Charles doesn't know what he's talking about.

He's a doctor. He fixes people, not problems . . . Call Uncle Martin at Tours and tell them to drive up here this afternoon.

But—

Just do it! I left; refused to let her see me weak inside. The problem was, I couldn't do it alone. I knew that island, and my voice wasn't strong enough to be heard by my uncles without baritone behind it.

So I fumbled through my backpack for Mr. Petion's business card and left a message with his secretary for him and Mr. Hill to *please, come* to Godwyn.

Chapter 26

AND THEY DID COME: Hill and Petion. As asked.

Uncle Charles and Uncle Martin waited until it was almost dark; pulled up the drive fast, as though they were in charge, had more important matters to attend to. The Pascals and their posturing; it's so obnoxious.

I rolled my eyes at Mr. Hill and Mr. Petion, looked at my watch. But we rose immediately, all four of us, from our seats on the front porch—my mom under strict orders not to say a word because she'd just set them off, squander what little sunlight we had left.

Uncle Martin, the wise guy, mentioned to his brother as they exited the Four-Runner, *Charles, I neglected to tell you. Jean has hired herself a pair of bodyguards.*

Good afternoon, gentlemen. Uncle Charles was not as amused as Uncle Martin. He would rather have bullied my mother out of Godwyn in private. Family matters.

But he had a mother to bury, earth to move to do so.

Mr. Hill and Mr. Petion nodded their hellos to my uncles; they already knew the plan: map out a path to the burial plot from Grampy's old access road, draw it up on the survey, and file it with the recorder's office in Bato before I left the island. Lock my uncles into a contract.

My mom will grant the family a right-of-way up the hill from the access road to the graves. All this fighting is unnecessary. I attempted a tone as patronizing as the one I was sure to hear back.

But I missed my mark. Uncle Charles was far more practiced. *Jean. You have this all wrong. We are not the enemy. Godwyn has been a family house since long before you were born. And it will remain that way . . . Perhaps it is we who have been at fault, in failing to instill in you the loyalty to this family that we have. Your mummy will never have to worry about a place to live in Baobique. You know that.*

He just didn't get it and he was wasting our time. I looked to Uncle Martin, incredulous to find myself turning to him as the voice of reason.

Uncle Martin. My mom has title now. That is not in dispute.

Mr. Hill backed me up: *She's right, Martin.*

Uncle Martin listened to the man he'd called the day before in panic, to find Susan for Granny, when he'd thought she still had a chance. He could concede to Hill, not to me. *Let's hear them out, Charles.*

Uncle Martin, Hill, and Petion all dressed for town, we piled into the Four-Runner, two too many, and backtracked down the drive to the access road.

My mom managed to maintain an uncomfortable silence until Uncle Martin passed too close to her plum tree. But that did it. *Martin! Watch the damn tree. You did that just to spite me. You'd level my whole house just to beat me down, if Jean weren't here.*

He did do it on purpose. That's just his nature, to push and push and push until he gets at the nerve, gets his reaction.

Oh, Sophie, be quiet! You're getting your little house. Be happy and shut your mouth.

Stop it! Both of you! Now I was screaming, too. The car much too small to contain us like this, Uncle Martin parked it in the middle of the access road and we all spilled out into deep red mud.

The light was going.

Mr. Hill pointed a long arm up the slope in the direction of the graves. *Here, cut in from the plum tree toward the pomerack.*

We'd walked the route already, before Uncle Martin and Uncle Charles arrived. The slope could support a narrow road, skirting the western border, roughly parallel to the existing access road.

No! Leave the plum tree! My mom, in high gear, not helping us at all on this grade.

We're leaving the plum tree! I screamed at her, hoping to drown her out.

Uncle Charles was obstinate, having lost one battle already. *That way is too steep. It will never hold.*

Yes, it will. We'll angle along this way, I pointed, *hug the existing road.*

But he wasn't listening to me, my voice useless in all that wind. A storm was kicking up again, out at sea.

I looked to Mr. Hill; he continued, led us up the slope and through the trees we marked earlier—the grapefruits, the coconuts—along the croton hedge to the crest, then straight to the plot. We pulled ourselves through in dwindling light, collected scratches and pricks from hidden thorns in thick, thick bush. By the time we reached the graves, it was completely dark.

This is going to work, I demanded toward my uncles, both with arms folded tight to their chests. As if demanding made it so.

The road will hold, Martin, Mr. Hill assured him.

I am against this. This would never be happening if George were still here. Uncle Charles, a child losing control.

Uncle Martin spoke to the ground as he addressed his brother. *But he's not here anymore, Charles. George is gone. And Mama's gone . . .*

As Granny and Uncle Charles lost their grip on Godwyn, Uncle Martin's hand grew stronger, steadied. That year had taken first his older brother, then his mother. He had never in his life had to be the Uncle George, until now. He looked my way. *This family needs a bridge. And the road will do . . . Jean, if you come to my office in Port Commons early enough tomorrow morning, we can draft the right-of-way before my court appearances.*

Everyone grew quiet. The winds had shifted along with our alliances. The fight let out of all of us, leaving behind just a sadness, deep as the night was dark.

We could bury Granny in two days' time.

Only as we walked back toward the house, sticky with aftermath, did I notice the porch light and her Subaru; Susan waiting for us to return.

Chapter 27

I CAN LEAVE IN TWO DAYS, was all I could think as we approached the house; Uncle Martin and Uncle Charles filing off to retrieve the Four-Runner from the mud in the access road; Messrs. Hill and Petion gone ahead to welcome Susan, like conquering heroes after a hard day's battle.

My mom and I stayed behind, walked a bit slower than the rest. Personally, I was in no hurry for the night's second confrontation. I dragged myself toward Susan.

Mom, I asked, more to look busy than anything else, *who is Marcus Greene? Do you know him?*

Isn't he the man that's dating Susan?

Dating?

Well, whatever it is you call it these days . . .

Like my mom, I had spent many years of my life alone. Much of the time I, too, felt as if I was waiting for someone to come along and complete me the way she lay in bed all those years when I was young, waiting for someone like Harold to make her whole, shutting her eyes to me and what the two of us could have had, just by ourselves.

There in the dark, she whispered to me about Susan's lover. *He's a freshman in the Assembly. One of the O.O.F.I. representatives trying to link all the islands together with one voice. They tell us that's the only way to gain international respect. People are saying he'll be the island's answer in a few years, just like George was, and Hill, in their time.*

Is he a lawyer?

No, I don't think so . . . He's some type of engineer. Came back from London last year for a political career. I hear he and Susan are becoming quite an item.

I took her arm, held her to a stop, not rough, just incredulous. *Mom, I can't believe you didn't tell me this earlier. Don't you know how I feel about her?* I said it soft enough so the others wouldn't hear, only loud enough for my mom.

Well, that's none of my business, Jean. Is it?

Not a question; I'd nothing to say, responded silently, with as few tears as possible. But I was glad for the dark, so no one could see me wipe my face dry.

My mom and I never talked about my lovers. In my mind, I always told myself it was because no one important enough had come along yet.

Things were changing so fast, it wasn't just the darkness making it hard to see.

We reached the porch smiling wide and fake for the others.

Mr. Hill would not hear of letting us cook, proposed taking us all out to that Trinidadian's restaurant in Tete Queue; the *only* restaurant in Tete Queue. But Mr. Petion had some work to do for an early-morning audit in Bato, would catch a ride with the next passing car or truck along the windy road south. And my mom wanted to start preparing the house for Granny's funeral. Although it was common for me to see no one but family when I visited Baobique, my social obligations were expanding.

Mr. Hill left his daughter and me no choice. Plan B was take-out curry in Susan's Port Commons apartment.

Before we left, we made sure the house was locked up tight: shutters closed, padlocks clicked, one dog in, one out.

I would walk over to Uncle Martin's office in the morning, from Susan's apartment, to draft the right-of-way.

Chapter 28

I WAS LEARNING HOW A LIFE MARKS TIME IN ERAS, not hours; saw my arms inch along, like a clock, in their revolution. By measure I am slow to learn, hold on to heavy luggage, like my mother and her too many bags at my apartment in Oakland, come to stay for as long as it took to send me packing, back to Baobique to anchor title to Godwyn beneath her feet.

I could do it. I could face Susan. She drove us to Port Commons; Mr. Hill gone ahead to pick up the curry. I looked out the window, felt like a child being driven to school.

I hated that I couldn't drive myself. Not on those roads. Especially at night, I lacked confidence on the left side.

We drove in silence the entire trip, neither of us anxious to go where we had to that night.

Mr. Hill must have called ahead from his cell phone to the restaurant and driven like a sixteen-year-old boy, because he pulled up with our dinner right after us in the parking lot of the Bank Royale, just underneath Susan's one-bedroom.

Inside, he brought us the curry: goat and chicken. And roti, to wrap it in. He also brought plastic forks and paper plates, having had the misfortune of trying to find such things in his daughter's apartment on prior occasions. He shook his head back and forth in domestic disapproval. Susan rolled her eyes on cue.

They were sweet, together like that. A team: father and daughter.

Mr. Hill offered me a plate of curry, placed his hand on my shoulder, winced at the way I butchered the pronunciation of *roti*, constitutionally incapable of keeping the *t* a *t*, repeatedly making it a *d: rodi*. We all gave up on that one. Susan's touch, soft and confident, came from him.

We avoided direct eye contact, made light with her father and the ease of his company; he was, simply, a good man.

After dinner, we talked about how things were changing. Baobique missed the reins of a strong leader; bucked yokeless like a wild horse in a crowded room. Uncle George and Prime Minister Hill were alike in that way; even though they had stood at opposite poles, they took care to aim for the long run.

The island was in need of proper guidance. But to look around, there were few individuals with the necessary foresight and charisma to do the job. And those few, still too young to hold tight the leads. So it was all petty fighting, petty fighting.

Just like my family, I joked. The analogy too stark to ignore. We laughed, but not really.

Susan was quiet, looked down at her plate. None of us mentioned her Marcus, a likely successor to our uncles' old thrones.

Mr. Hill assured me, *It's the same all over, Jean. You should have seen my brothers and sisters fight over Archie's share of the Hill estate.*

Really? I was shocked. *But you all seem so calm.*

Ha! Susan broke her silence.

We all laughed. Really.

So maybe I can feel a little less ashamed—about being a Pascal.

Ah, but that is the true mark of a Pascal—placing shame on others. Susan cut to the heart with surgical precision.

Our laughter stopped. Cold in its tracks.

It was time for Mr. Hill to leave.

* * *

On the white lattice along the stairway leading to Susan's apartment, two little lizards crisscrossed paths. One tilted its head backward, blew up its throat. The other bobbed its head up and down, up and down.

We waited until we were back inside her apartment and the doors were safely shut.

Then we went at it. Fast and hard. Voices raised.

When, in God's name, Susan, were you going to mention Marcus? I started, claimed the moral high ground from the get-go.

I was waiting, Jean, until you, maybe, decided to answer one of my dozen damn letters. She claimed it back.

We retreated for a moment, regrouped, went again.

I lowered my voice, metered my words. *Do you have any idea how much it hurt to see you with him like that today? What were you thinking?*

It is a qualitatively different kind of abandonment when a woman leaves a woman for a man. Things are different in theory than they are in real life. I would've had no problem with Susan sleeping with men if she wasn't my lover. I knew this was unfair, a bigotry of sorts. But it was, simply, how I felt.

She could have done anything else, but this—this I couldn't take.

She let me continue. So I did. *Since I arrived, I've fooled myself into thinking that you and I might be falling in love; that this past year was just one bad leg of a relationship that never really ended. But the truth is, we don't really know each other at all . . . Maybe we're just two completely incompatible people.*

Neither of us angry anymore, Susan spoke, explained. *I didn't tell you about Marcus because I wanted to give us a chance first. Jean, you shut me out of your life for a very long time. Somewhere during all those months of waiting for your reply, I stopped needing an answer. Marcus was here for me. And honestly, he's much easier to handle than you are. You make such mountains out of molehills sometimes. Such a Pascal.*

Thank you for that.

I am not finished. She wasn't amused. Continued. *Marcus is better to me than you ever have been. He is steady. And reliable. And affectionate. And I should want him at least as much as I do you. But right now I don't know what I want. You confuse me.*

She left me an opening and I jumped straight through. *Susan, I love you. I am sorry I've been such an idiot. Let me show you, I can be so much better . . . Come back to California with me. You've considered it before . . .* Ugh. Probably not a good idea to have brought up that letter.

Right. She sighed; then silence.

I'd lost her. When would I learn not to lead with my fists?

For a second I felt the desire to flee, but truth be told, I'd rather have been there fighting with Susan than anywhere else.

My grandmother is being buried at Godwyn the day after next. I'll be on the afternoon flight out, was all I could say.

This is how I cut myself open: the rough edge of a coconut, crushed for milk against the rock at Granny's beach, pressed tight against my wrist—I pulled, knowing Grampy was wrong and the sea could not possibly heal such a wound.

I will not lose you, J. Not twice. She was crying.

And, apparently, so was I. I felt like I was in San Francisco, not Baobique; so thick with fog I couldn't see the bridge.

I'd sleep on the couch. Forego the mosquito netting.

Some time later, the telephone rang us awake.

I'm always on call, Susan explained, stumbling into the living room for the phone. She answered, *This is Dr. Hill.*

But she brought the receiver to the couch, handed it to me.

I heard static, and then an apology: *Jean, I'm so sorry. I'm so sorry to bother you. Your office gave me your mother's number. She gave me this one. Something's happened. I just need to talk.* It was Cynthia.

The morning had caught her still in bed, Sadie at an overnight with a YMCA playgroup learning social skills, when the phone rang.

Collect call from Linda Thompson. Do you accept the charges?

Yes.

Cynthia?

Linda, where are you?

At the police station.

What's the matter?

I was attacked. Voice cracking.

Are you okay?

No.

Cynthia'd pulled on Linda's black polar fleece sweatpants from the way-back of the dresser drawer. She stumbled into their Volvo and ran the three stoplights leading to the station house. A fire engine waiting in front, lights flashing. A man and a woman sitting on the front steps.

Two paramedics and a cop stooped over Linda. One trying to get her to sign a waiver, one trying to take her blood pressure, and one apparently just taking up space.

Cynthia'd knelt, put her hand on Linda's knee right in front of everybody, a move she mightn't have done when they were still together.

What happened?

I was attacked, Linda answered.

By who?

Those people, pointing to the couple on the stairs.

Why?

And Linda began to cry.

It had started with the dogs. Theirs and Linda's, none of whom were on a leash and all of whom had wanted to sniff each other. So they had. The couple's dog, busy, would not respond to their calls. They yelled at Linda for not having hers on a leash. She'd reminded them that their dog was also unleashed. The man threatened to hurt Linda's dog and she told him he was crazy.

Fucking dyke! Bitch! Fucking whore! The metal clasp of the man's leash came down on her head first, it's nylon strap cutting a gash across her face. And then she was on the ground, in the dirt, under the woman; the woman straddling Linda, her husband punching and kicking and spitting. Then the woman put her face to Linda's breast and bit down, hard as she could.

If you touch my wife I'll kill you, you fucking dyke!

They'd let her up.

Okay. It's over, he said.

Not until I talk to a cop! Linda screamed.

They jumped on her again.

This time she was able to shout.

But no one came.

Linda had lain underneath. The woman's full weight on her chest. She'd lain as they punched, kicked, and spat. She spat back.

Again, they let her up. She followed them, asking everyone along the way, along the exercise path, for a cell phone to call the police. Everyone looking back blank. The fifth person she'd asked, a frail elderly woman, had taken pity and given her a phone. As Linda called the police, the couple started walking toward the station.

She returned the woman's phone and collected their little dog, who had started to run to Cynthia's, they assumed, to get help. He never would have made it. He got so lost in the tall grass along the dunes. By the time Linda got to the station, the man had already burst through the front door, announcing, *My wife's been attacked!*

Linda followed him in, bruised and welted.

The police officer was absolutely useless. *Seems like a case of he said/she said.* He took a report from Linda against the couple, and a report from the couple against Linda, while looking at their unblemished skin, Linda's welts, bruises, and bite mark. A paramedic suggested she go to the emergency room, although the waiver she'd signed released him from actually having to drive her.

Can I use the phone? she asked.

There's a pay phone over there.

Cynthia had driven her to the hospital. The attending physician said Linda would be feeling effects for some time. *Severe trauma*, she'd said. Prescribed a pill for shock, and a tetanus booster. Within the next seventy-two hours, Linda would need a hepatitis check, an HIV test, and another one in six months. She should not have unprotected sex until the test results came back negative. She would need to call the district attorney, who had the power to court order the woman to have her blood drawn and tested for communicable diseases.

There was no mention of Cara that evening.

I told Cynthia I'd be home *as soon as I can*, and that *everything is going to be okay.* I promised. I told her to take care of herself, and Sadie, and Linda. *Keep safe. Keep yourselves safe*, I told her, and hung up.

The rain had come. It let down hard on the roof, mixed with the red clay of the roadside to make a mortar, walling me in. My breath shallow and fast.

J, come back. Susan sat beside me, circled her arm around my shoulder, dug her fingers deep into my curls. Held me.

Outside, *shhhhhhh*—the rain covered us in sheets.

Chapter 29

SUSAN AND I ROSE EARLY from our respective beds, took turns in the shower rinsing the stick of the night from our skin, went our separate ways: she to the clinic, me to Uncle Martin's office just blocks away along Port Commons' single street.

I let the mosquito bites on my legs itch without scratching as I walked. The mosquitoes knew I didn't belong in Baobique; drank their fill of me while they could. The longer I was there, the less I let them bother me. Their bites turned red and swelled on their own. Regardless of my actions, I'd scar.

By the time I arrived, Uncle Martin was already in. But he had a preliminary matter to deal with before we could turn our attention to Godwyn. He called in a young girl holding a thrashing sack by its top with a death grip to keep it closed. Something angry inside, jumping and scratching to get out. The girl cleaned the apartment complex he owned down the road. Uncle Martin turned to me and asked, *What would the criminal penalty be in the States for stealing a cat?*

A cat? I asked back, surprised at the question.

Yes. A cat.

Misdemeanor, probably, I hazarded a guess, shrugged it off.

Oh! Then it's okay. He turned to the girl, told her to *walk out past the river and let it go.*

The girl nodded, left, tight fists first—bag in grip—shut the door behind her with a thickly calloused foot.

Uncle Martin explained. *The tenant knows the rules. No cats allowed in the rental units.*

So why don't you just evict her? Unable to be alarmed anymore.

I want her money. I don't want her to leave. Just the cat.

I didn't raise a stink. And we moved on.

These two worlds of mine, Baobique and California, are simply irreconcilable. It is like comparing apples to oranges, or plums to coconuts. When I'm in San Francisco, Baobique scarcely exists for me. Yet there, I have no family, no context, no blood to remind me that I, too, have ties to this earth. In Baobique, it is literally the earth that tells me who I am, where I come from, and, very possibly, who I am still to be.

My uncle's generation was learning day by day that they were mortal. Who was left, if not me, to move us forward?

Let's get to work, I suggested.

And we did.

There are many ways to solve a problem. And while I'd take a written agreement over kidnapping a woman's cat any day, it is a weak family that turns to a contract to resolve its conflicts.

But Baobique is like an onion pulled up from the ground, always peeling off another layer: layers of mountains and the valleys running through them; layers of green, constantly shifting hues; layers of truth popping out here and there from behind fast-moving clouds; layers of hate. And love. Every time I'd think I'd figured it out, something different showed its face.

Uncle Martin picked up a pad of paper from a pile on his messy desk, cleared a space to write, and told me what I already knew. He pointed his index finger to my face, did not mince words. *This agreement*, he said, *will never see the inside of a courtroom.*

I didn't mention that threat was my only leverage to reel in my two uncles from those choppy waters.

Uncle Martin picked up his fancy fountain pen from England, dipped it in a jar of ink, got in one last jab: *I want you to know, Jean, this is a new low for the Pascals. I cannot believe it has come to this.*

I let that one pass, too, without response. But not really. To be honest, I agreed. I just placed fault at different feet in that particular instance.

No one starts out drafting a contract in the hopes of a suit. And everyone knows a family's laws are stronger than a court's. But sometimes, maybe, a contract can be a bridge between too many tired voices, hoarse from screaming. At least that was the plan.

It was up to me to set a cooperative tone. I gave Uncle Martin this: *Let's just be careful not to say anything we shouldn't.*

Fair enough.

He started writing, spoke each word as he completed it. *Right-of-Way: WHEREAS, the Pascal family wishes to preserve access to the burial plot of Dr. and Mrs. William Pascal, and their children, Sophie Pascal-Souza grants the Pascal family members an access road, no wider than twenty feet—*

No way, I stopped him. *Twenty feet is too wide. Ten feet in width is more than enough for a car.*

Ten feet, plus one foot on either side for drainage. It will need drainage. Uncle Martin did know about cutting roads.

Fine. Twelve feet in width. I was satisfied.

He continued, all business. I'd never seen him so focused—*no wider than twelve feet. To cut from the existing estate access road, to the burial plot—*

No. I could see what he was doing. Always pushing, Uncle Martin. So I demanded, *We need to map out the path as we walked it last night. So it's clear where to cut.*

Oh, I see. I see where you're going with this . . . Okay: no wider than twelve feet. To cut from the existing estate access road, to the burial plot, along the following path: cutting in at, and passing between, the two grapefruit trees along the eastern portion of the existing estate access road; continuing to, and proceeding left at, the first coconut tree; proceeding parallel to the existing access road, along its eastern edge—

Leave the croton hedge. And the segos, I reminded him.

As we reached the bottom of the last page, the end of the right-of-way, we were both completely at ease, hunched over Uncle Martin's desk: him writing, me watching his every pen stroke, stopping him, backtracking, reworking. The agreement was as rough as the port at Sommerset in the middle of the night. But I wasn't in San Francisco anymore. And rough worked in Baobique.

We looked at each other, smiled, hoped it would hold.

We still needed my mom's signature. But I could get that. If I had to reach under her pillow, place that pistol to her head, she'd sign. This was the best deal she'd get. And it was up to me to make it so. I knew what was best for her.

Yet Uncle Martin was still Uncle Martin—he was on the phone with contractors to cut the road even before it had been typed up.

I called my mom for a ride back to Godwyn from the waiting area.

If all went well, we'd bury Granny the next morning. And I'd be on the afternoon flight out.

Chapter 30

MY MOM PICKED ME UP from Uncle Martin's office in her jeep, had waiting: two bottles of water and a brown paper bag with two slices of fresh-baked banana bread, still warm from the old woman in Tete Queue.

I told her, *Uncle Martin will have the agreement typed up for you to sign before the funeral tomorrow. You don't have to worry anymore about Godwyn . . . It's over, Mom.*

What about the trees? Did you tell them he couldn't cut down any of the trees? He'll cut them, you know; he'll take out my whole yard if you let him.

Mom. Let go. It's over. This is as good as it gets. He's not going to cut any of the trees we talked about last night. Okay? Just accept it. Be happy, for Christ's sake. For once.

She couldn't, though. Finally, I saw that. Even though she didn't say anything more about it, her mind was going 'round and 'round, locked in conflict.

Granny's passing got my mom Godwyn. And the agreement we all negotiated for the right-of-way to the graves would hopefully quiet the family's stormy attitude about the whole situation, or at least downgrade it from hurricane level. I know I was needed there for that. I know I helped. But I wished I could untangle my mom's real troubles, the ones inside her head that take over now and then and knock her flat—with no small help from the people around her.

When she first called to tell me about Uncle George's death, she'd been distracted by the havoc such a large funeral service would wreak on her small plot of land. She'd wanted to buy torches, lace them between the sego lining her drive for the younger brother who'd passed in her arms. But it slipped her mind.

Before we cleared Port Commons, I asked her, *Maybe we could buy some of those torches and stake them for Granny?*

So we did.

Back at my mom's, I thought it would be a good idea to check in on Cynthia, to see how she and Linda were doing.

It was so incredibly surreal, sitting at the dining table, looking out at my mom starting to stake torches between the budding palms just in front of the bright orange flowers on the flamboyant tree; calling Cynthia in San Francisco to see how bad Linda's beating had been.

I dialed the numbers but Cynthia didn't answer. Their machine picked up with a recording of Sadie. A soft invitation to *please leave a message.*

I didn't, though. I placed my mom's receiver back in its rest before the end of the beep, certain only that I shouldn't intrude.

My mom and I passed the afternoon in her yard, worked with our hands, not our heads, to ready the torches for Granny and the rest of them, come tomorrow morning.

But Granny's funeral wouldn't be near the size of Uncle George's. I reminded her of that, repeatedly.

And in the dirt she loosened.

Did I ever tell you about your father's chicks? she asked.

There is a picture of my parents in Illinois at a party. They seem like, in their mid-twenties, babies themselves, but I know by that time they'd already had me, unpictured. My father is sitting on a couch between two women, laughing; my mother in a chair to the side, not. I don't know how many affairs my father had, how many more sisters or even brothers I might have had, had he not gotten an operation that made it medically impossible.

Chicks? I wasn't sure I wanted to know. *As in women?*

No. Chicks! Chicks! Baby chicks!

Oh God, I half-laughed. *No, you didn't.*

So she told me. *For months, all we ate was chicken. First I just baked it, or powdered it with white flour and fried it up in a little oil on the stove. But after a while, I started thinking hard: "How can I make this taste like something else?" Let me tell you, we ate sweet chicken, salty chicken, ketchup chicken. You name it, I put it on that chicken. Chicken with orange sauce, mango sauce, coconut.*

You still see them selling those chicks at the airport; cardboard crates of them piled in their vans. That's where your father got the idea for his. He bought a pallet of them straight from Trinidad. He thought he could make a side business, while he taught during the day. Got enough orders in the first few weeks to sell the whole batch when the hens reached maturity. We fed those chicks by hand, you know, with eyedroppers from Grampy's office: fortified cow's milk, canned, like we drank ourselves, and farinha. Those birds ate better than most Baobiquens.

But when the time came for him to sell, none of the people who'd placed orders came through. Not a one. It was George, you know. Just to be spiteful. Trading favors in secret to stop the sales; showing his true colors even then: politicking at nineteen. Your father thought he was something else for winning me, Dr. Pascal's daughter, on nothing but a teacher's salary. Nothing but a pauper, your father; that's what he was. George reminded him of that.

* * *

We were sitting in a booth of cracked red pleather, eating breakfast at the back of a Phoenix diner, the first time I realized my father saw the world as one big conspiracy—intentionally picking its victims.

Eggs over-medium with hash browns and lots of ketchup; toast, uneaten.

Before the divorce, my dad was a microbiology professor teaching medical students and earning less, with my mom and me to support, than his students paid for a year's tuition.

By the time I was in college, he'd gone to medical school himself and become a doctor, grossing multiples of his previous salary, which made him happier, but beyond that hadn't changed him much at all.

Second semester sophomore year, I needed somewhere to go for winter break. I visited him because he paid for the plane ticket.

He likes to speak loudly in public places, especially if the things he's saying are things people normally don't.

He likes to shock.

Over eggs sophomore year, he told me what he thought about AIDS.

The American people don't know this, but believe me, AIDS is an international government plan to wipe out the faggots . . . Listen to me—you don't think I know what I'm talking about?

My father, the benevolent physician, continued, *When I was in microbiology research, I almost worked for the Department of Defense . . . Biological warfare, Jean. They have scientists working day and night. They tested it in the Caribbean first, the fuckers. Now it's domestic strategy.* His doctoral thesis had been on blue-green algae. A lay person might have missed the connection.

I finished my eggs with nods and grunts, vowed to start the day as if it were any other.

* * *

My mom finished her story about my dad and his chicks as she stabbed the soft earth with an unlit torch. *After that, your father would stop at nothing to get off this island. Nothing. And he took his turn on me: always needing to remind me he was on top—even if I was a Pascal.*

I hazarded a guess at her motives for telling me that story. *So I guess Baobique isn't for everyone after all. Maybe it's only for real Pascals.*

She looked me straight in the eye. *You may have your father's name, Jean Souza, but you are my child . . . And I have the papers to prove it.*

She was right. I am her child. I don't belong to my father at all. He gave me up without even a hearing; just a signature.

The court papers read very simply:

Upon the stipulation of the natural father, IT IS HEREBY ORDERED: that the permanent care, custody, control, and education of the minor child, Jean Souza, is vested in Sophie Pascal-Souza, the natural mother.

My father stipulated away his legal ties to me the day after I caught him in the kitchen with my mom, broken dishes on the floor and that fist shattering more than he ever could have imagined. Maybe I had chosen sides after all, that night, at the bottom of the back staircase. Maybe he saw my choice right that second, in the look I gave him—his own green eyes staring back at him. Because he sure showed me. The next day leaving us. And giving me to my mom. There was no fight in open court. No hearing. No argument back or forth. Just a single civil agreement.

Stipulations are reserved for matters unworthy of con-tention, for issues one wishes to leave behind and is therefore willing to concede; in order to move on to more important matters.

Sometimes we say things in a contract that should never be said. Sometimes just the telling of unspeakable words leaves us thinned to pulp—and dried; like the paper they're written on; turning blood to tissue, over time. Easily torn.

Even though I waited for Susan's call all afternoon—pulling the telephone out onto the front porch, stretching the cord a bit more, perhaps, than I should have—she never rang. I knew I could have had her paged at the clinic, but didn't.

By evening, my mom and I had long finished in the yard and already eaten a light dinner of pasta and avocado pear, the sun gone down. Susan's Subaru drove up from the road.

From the porch, I could see she looked tired, as if she'd either had a very long day at work, or just received some very bad news. Hard to tell which.

Hello, J, she opened. Softly.

Hey . . . I wasn't sure you were going to stop by tonight . . . I'm glad you did. I sat on my hands, so as not to lead with them. *Have you eaten?*

No. I've been busy all afternoon. And I didn't want to miss you tonight. So I came straight up from Bato.

Hang on. I'll get you a plate. I left her on the porch, ran into the kitchen, asked my mom, clearing dishes next to her window, the one that looks past the cliffs to the ocean, if there was anything left from dinner. She said she'd find something.

I returned to the porch with some tea to tide her over.

Susan asked, *Jean, do you know what I did today?*

No. What? Half hoping she'd tell me she'd stopped seeing Marcus. But I was off, way off.

I delivered a baby, partially breached, in the parking lot of the clinic, because there wasn't enough space inside. I should have had, at the very least, one assistant. But it was just me and Mrs. Bruce, out there on the tarish, for three and a half hours in the midday sun.

It had been hot—just staking those torches, enough to send my mom and me in every twenty minutes for water.

Wow. What happened? Did everything turn out okay?

She sighed. Patient with her own exasperation.

That's not the point, J. The point is that Mrs. Bruce gave birth to her second child on gravel this afternoon because we lacked resources for even a simple bed.

Wait! Mrs. Bruce? I know her husband. He has a bad eye, right? Everything was something there. There are no loose threads in Baobique, I swear.

Yes. He cut it in a political riot some years back. But what does that have to do with anything? She couldn't follow my tracks.

I blurted, *They lost their first baby,* proud of my knowledge.

Yes . . . But not this one. She rerouted me. Continued, *After the delivery, I was so angry I drove down to Bato to the new Prime Minister's office and threatened to leave the clinic if we didn't get proper funding after the next Assembly meeting.*

Again, *Wow . . . What'd he say?*

We set up a meeting for next week. I am one of only five physicians on the island. It would matter a great deal if I left. He'll listen.

Mmmm, I worried. I knew where we were headed.

My mom brought out some avocado and a sardine sandwich, brought a slow smile to the heavy lips through which Susan spoke. *I spent the rest of the day with Marcus.*

I felt like such a child, spending the day there with my mom, drinking juice squeezed from the grip of someone else's hand and digging in the dirt, while Susan battled Baobique's most pressing matters, the razor edge of life itself.

But I did know how to behave as an adult. So I did my best to listen. I asked, *What did you and Marcus talk about?*

She laughed a bit. He made her laugh. *Everything*, she answered. *Mrs. Bruce, the Prime Minister, the clinic, Baobique, and whether there is any hope left, any real chance of survival for our island . . .*

That wasn't really what I meant.

But she knew, continued, *Mostly we talked about how a person can be completely in love with two people at once. And if it's possible, really, to keep both in one's heart.*

This was hard. This was really hard. She'd opened my heart and there was, it seemed, no closing it back. I wanted to help. I owed her that. And an open heart must be able to hurt. So I gathered up the kind of courage I'd only ever seen in Susan.

I asked, *The meeting next week about the clinic. Is there anything my uncles can do to help with the funding? I mean, the hospital's Grampy's namesake, after all . . .*

She wouldn't be following me back to Oakland. Susan belonged here. We both knew it. We'd just needed a little help reaching certainty.

She took my hand.

J, she whispered.

Yes, I followed.

How do I show you that I am with you for the long haul? she asked.

Just like this . . . I answered. *By showing me that what I need most isn't always what I think.*

We forced our smiles, swallowed back the lumps rising in our throats, kept whispering.

I love you, Jean.

I love you, too . . . Susan?

Yes, J.

Will you come to Granny's funeral tomorrow?

Of course.

Susan?

Yes, J.

Invite Marcus.

Okay . . . Thank you . . . J?

Yes.

I'm too tired to drive home . . .

And we laughed, really; slept the night's long hours tight together under the mosquito netting next door to my mom.

Chapter 31

MORNING BROKE CLEAR AND WIDE through the open shutters in my mom's second bedroom. She must have come in while Susan and I were still asleep and unlocked them.

At breakfast, though, she didn't mention seeing us lying intertwined. Even though Susan and I had clung together rapt in something different than sex, my mom didn't know that. As always, she averted her eyes from that part of my life.

It's one thing for me to be gay, in theory, in San Francisco, another to bring it home to Baobique. Granted, it would have been easier to push back on the issue there in her dining room if I really *did* have a partner. It's hard for me to criticize my mom for ignoring a life I'd yet to create.

I'd always assumed that I would come out to my extended family one day. But I'd assumed that day would be more volitional than it actually was: Uncle Martin, Mr. Williams, Susan, and myself, in the dirt out back, over aging roots.

Thing is, the kind of person I've been, I'm not too sure I ever would have gotten around to telling anyone there the truth about myself if I hadn't been caught. I would have avoided the whole thing if I could have. Maybe it was a blessing in disguise, because it seemed to me, even with Uncle George and Granny gone, even with Susan's decision to stay in Baobique with Marcus where she belongs, I felt my world had grown, not shrunk.

Maybe love is bigger than I thought; big as an ocean, not just a bathroom sink. And maybe it's like my family: as big as I choose to make it.

Susan was in the kitchen staring out the window to the bright morning blue of the water far below, talking to my mom about her crotons, when the phone rang. Just Auntie Lil, checking in.

There was only one hitch with the right-of-way: it lacked specific reference to the plum tree. My mom didn't want to sign without it, but she did because I pressed the issue. Two copies. I wanted one for safe keeping, and the closest photocopy machine was all the way in Port Commons.

They didn't have to dig the hole too big this time, because Uncle Charles had Granny cremated in Bato while Uncle Martin and I were drafting up the right-of-way.

This way she'll take up less space, he'd explained. The plot is small, and no one was getting any younger. Soon enough there'd be another, and another, and another of us to join them.

He lowered her in, in the only bronze urn from the undertaker. Since Granny had no body anymore, just ash, it didn't matter which way her feet faced. East. Or west. Uncle Charles could take comfort in that.

Granny lived as Grampy's wife for less than thirty of her ninety-five years. A fraction of her life. But her marker would bear his name so that the future would remember her as his: *Mrs. William Pascal.*

If a man and a woman are one, what happens when they create a family? How many does that make?

What about a woman and a woman? Must they always be two?

And which is better? One or two?

During the ceremony, it sprinkled. But not hard. *Just the sun washing himself.* Or God, maybe, tinkling.

Marcus came with orchids from the nursery near Milieu, but stood in back, present and patient. Messrs. Hill and Petion helped my uncles with the heavy work of the digging up and refilling of earth.

The birds sang. And a gentle breeze licked clean our gathering. Tired as I was from the week's ordeal, part of me wanted to lie down with my grandparents and Uncle George—let the earth have me, too.

Before I left Godwyn for the airport, I picked four guavas off the tree in front; left one for Granny, one for Grampy, one for Uncle George, and kept one for myself.

While my uncles were busy with something else, I pressed an envelope into Mr. Hill's palm; asked him and Mr. Petion to record the right-of-way at the registrar on their return to Bato that afternoon. *Just to keep Uncle Martin honest,* I whispered softly, winking myself into their confidence. They nodded back, co-conspirators who'd made their way into my heart.

I hugged them goodbye as I would old uncles, not new friends.

It was easier to say goodbye to my family—Uncle Charles, Uncle Martin, Auntie Clara, Granny, Grampy, Uncle George, and even my mom—than it was for me to leave Susan, return to the barren walls of my studio.

We'd planned a short sea bath at Tours beach on the way to Beckford Hall—my mom, Susan, and me—to relax before my long journey home.

We passed Granny's house in mom's jeep, Uncle Martin's bright white button-downs on the clothesline, blowing in the wind.

We passed Polly and Eugene on their porch, waved them off without stopping.

My mom parked the jeep to the side of the road and we walked down the twisty red clay path to the beach as she explained something to us—urgent but of no immediate importance.

In the water, a school of silverfish.

At the airport, I asked my mom if she and I could say our good-byes at the car. And we did, embracing for just the slightest moment longer than usual.

The salt from the sea at my family's beach still white and chalky on my skin, Susan followed me in.

There was a bat, small, black, and fleshy, hanging by the air conditioner in the waiting area, simply fascinating all the American tourists. But Susan rolled her eyes at them, so I didn't get to look at it quite as long as I would have liked.

I was ready to be somewhere else. She helped me with my backpack, all the way out to the tarmac, hugged me goodbye at the foot of the plane. Tighter 'round my ribs, though, was the loss, hewn to my chest, that stayed with me even after her release. There were no winds. Except for my crying, that last leg was as quiet as just after a hurricane, when the hermit crab crawls side-ways out of its cave.

Also from AKASHIC BOOKS

WITH OR WITHOUT YOU BY LAUREN SANDERS
317 PAGES, A TRADE PAPERBACK ORIGINAL, $14.95

"A wickedly crafted whydunit . . . Sanders shows a surprising ability to simultaneously make you feel infuriated with and sorry for her borderline-schizo heroine."
—*Entertainment Weekly*

"Sanders's vibrant, vigorous second novel is a sendup of America's obsession with pop culture, B-list celebrities, and prison life . . . In lyrical, potent prose, Sanders navigates the terrain of loneliness, obsession and desperation with the same skillful precision as her vulnerable, calculating protagonist."
—*Publishers Weekly* (starred review)

BLACK MARKS BY KIRSTEN DINNALL HOYTE
274 PAGES, A TRADE PAPERBACK ORIGINAL, $14.95

"*Black Marks* employs the techniques of the old-fashioned quest narrative in exploring the extremely complex circumstances of modern American life. Georgette Collins is forced to confront, within herself, class and racial tensions, sexual and cultural choices, in her attempt to better understand herself and to learn and claim the sacred 'true-true name' inherited from her Jamaican ancestors. This is a much-needed contribution to contemporary American fiction."
—James A. McPherson, Pulitzer-winning author of *Elbow Room*

SOUTHLAND BY NINA REVOYR
*WINNER OF A LAMBDA LITERARY AWARD AND A FERRO-GRUMLEY AWARD; A *LOS ANGELES TIMES* BEST-SELLER
348 PAGES, A TRADE PAPERBACK ORIGINAL, $15.95

"What makes a book like *Southland* resonate is that it merges elements of literature and social history with the propulsive drive of a mystery, while evoking Southern California as a character, a key player in the tale. Such aesthetics have motivated other Southland writers, most notably Walter Mosley."
—*Los Angeles Times*

"If Oprah still had her book club, this novel likely would be at the top of her list . . . With prose that is beautiful, precise, but never pretentious . . ."
—*Booklist* (starred review)

JOHN CROW'S DEVIL BY MARLON JAMES
226 PAGES, HARDCOVER, $19.95

"Set in James's native Jamaica, this dynamic, vernacular debut sings of the fierce battle between two flawed preachers . . . an exciting read."
—*Publishers Weekly*

"*John Crow's Devil* is the finest and most important first novel I've read in years. Marlon James's writing brings to mind early Toni Morrison, Jessica Hagedorn, and Gabriel García Márquez."
—Kaylie Jones, author of *A Soldier's Daughter Never Cries*

SOME OF THE PARTS BY T COOPER
*A BARNES & NOBLE DISCOVER GREAT NEW WRITERS PROGRAM SELECTION
264 PAGES, A TRADE PAPERBACK ORIGINAL, $14.95

The novel that's changing the way we define "family." The Osbournes, Sopranos, and Eminem are only "some of the parts" that make up the whole story of the new American family.

"A wholly original novel that's both discomforting and compelling to read."
—*San Francisco Chronicle*

BECOMING ABIGAIL BY CHRIS ABANI
*AN *ESSENCE MAGAZINE* BOOK CLUB SELECTION
122 PAGES, A TRADE PAPERBACK ORIGINAL, $11.95

"[A] powerful, harrowing work . . . *Becoming Abigail* is more compressed and interior [than *GraceLand*], a poetic treatment of terror and loneliness . . . It may lack the earlier novel's scope, but its isolating strategy, its sharp focus on the devastation of one young woman, has a deeper kind of resonance."
—*New York Times Book Review*
